OUTSIDE SOMEWHERE, A LAMP BURNS

SHIVCHARAN JAGGI KUSSA

WhiteFalcon Publishing

www.whitefalconpublishing.com

OUTSIDE SOMEWHERE A LAMP BURNS
Shivcharan Jaggi Kussa

www.whitefalconpublishing.com

ISBN - 978-93-89932-12-6

The names, places, and events mentioned in this novel are all imaginary and have no connection whatsoever with any actual names, places, or events. If any name, place, or event happens to resemble with one, the writer or the publisher is not responsible for the same.

Special Thanks:

My friend Sanjiv Kapoor

Preface

Outside Somewhere, A Lamp Burns
Author: Shivcharan Jaggi Kussa

Punjabi Literature has had its fair share of good books and bad books. Sadly most of the writers of the Punjab who choose to write in Punjabi are either limited in their knowledge of the world beyond Village Literature or are clearly limited in exposure to modern world techniques and so are unable to capture the familiar in a fresh way or one up to international standards. This is not true of Jaggi Kussa and his book, Barhi Koee Balda Deeva – Outside, Somewhere, A Lamp Burns. One can tell that Shivcharan Jaggi Kussa is well read and a deft hand at plot and characterisation. I assume that he has read Punjabi translations of international literature, such as Tolstoy. Although Shivcharan Jaggi Kussa lives in London, and thus is world wise, he always keeps his subjects close to his readership's heart. Despite my criticism above of other Punjabi writers, the readers are mainly going to only be interested in local matters, and that is what Shivcharan Jaggi Kussa does. This is a time where Punjabi Literature is at a crossroads, where the old guard, writers and readers alike, are completely out of touch with India's new generation, their interest and ambitions. The threat to Punjabi of this is a staid set of stories and the established writers patting themselves on the back, producing a deluge of old hat, and fooling the public in thinking that they are somehow great writers. They are not. And nowadays the public is not fooled. They simply switch from Punjabi to Hindi, or more likely, English, with books such as Harry Potter. There is a growing market for the same in Punjabi, but aside from the block from the old guard, a tragic danger is the Indian publishing system that fails to pay royalties, expects new writers to pay for their work, which any foolish printer can do, and have no idea when it comes to editing, of correct Punjabi Idiom, or use of unusual to Punjabi, but perfectly acceptable techniques to the rest of the world, such as not using commas, or periods, when trying to show a protagonist running out of breath, and making the reader do the same. This is a technique seen used by Roop Dhillon quite often, whilst writers like Des Raj Kali tackle social issues that Indians would rather stay blind to. Shivcharan Jaggi Kussa is not quite part of this wave, but certainly uses modern techniques that make Nanak Singh, Gurdial Singh and Amrita Pritam look so out of date. The main thing is Shivcharan Jaggi Kussa's stories have pace, excitement and deal with social issues that others are afraid of or just incapable of. In many ways the front cover, with its white Greek Tragic Mask merging into a carcass like rib cage, captures the mood of the novel, "Barhi Kohee Balda Deeva" (BKBD). BKBD follows the tragic life of a group of Sikhs from West Punjab, now Pakistan, who against any wish of their own are forced to leave for the new promised land, India, where instead of finding peace and acceptance, over time are abused, harassed and eventually tortured, killed or mistreated, for no other reason, than that they are Sikhs. A group, Including Gyani Ji, Amli, Santu and Gurmukh Singh who along with their families are forced out of their home village, because it is now Muslim only Pakistan, to a Refugee Camp, where with thousands of others they are forced to wait weeks on end, to be allocated land, in the new country, taken from Muslims forced into Pakistan, in compensation for their old homes. Tragedy begins here, as day in day out, they are mistreated by the camp Organisers and two "In Charges", and finally given land, with one not sent to the same village. As a result they agree to always meet at Amritsar every year.

Although this does not happen, Gyanni Puran Singh enthusiastically manages to take all the layabouts, druggies and loafers from their newly allocated village away from their poor lives, into the Khalsa, by visiting the place annually. This habit soon gets him in trouble with the evil village Mayor, Jaggar Singh, who is jealous of the new arrival and labels him a Terrorist. Thus begins a new tragedy. Shivcharan Jaggi Kussa created many characters in this short but epic novel, all who are well rounded and play their part in the ensuing and engaging tragedy. From Melo, a mad girl in the camp, rape victim of the partition, to Kulbir, 4 decades later to be killed in vile anti-Sikh attacks post assassination of Indira Gandhi. At different stages of the novel, one those mentioned so far become the focal point, thus lead characters, whilst the other protagonists fade to the background, until their experiences become relevant not only to plot, but reflecting the social ills placed upon the characters lives. Jaggar is sly and never exposed to anyone but the reader, infuriating us, as we can see what is to unfold, but the characters are blind o it. He is supported ably by a Police force more corrupt and evil than the criminals in the west, and a million miles away from the English Bobby. These are in the form of Thanadars Brar and Jag Singh who apparently torture and pick on Sikhs because it is an unspoken Government policy from Delhi. This is only ever implied, as Shivcharan Jaggi Kussa assumes the readers knowledge of twentieth century Punjab. In the early stages of the novel we meet the protagonists named above, just as Partition hits India. It is clear that they do not want to leave their homeland for a new India, and think the idea of Pakistan is crazy, and no good to anyone but the Leaders. Alas events build up, and communal violence around religious identity erupts. Santu loses two sons. His wife, who also loved her Muslim neighbours, can not bear to part. Whereas most Partition novels deal with the atrocities of the same, this one focuses on the treatment of the refuges. When the In charge finally does allocate homes from them, we are shown how on entering the new home, it is cold and alien. Yet by the end of the novel, the home is full of memories which are bitter sweet for Gurmukh, in contrast. One of the wonderful techniques used by Shivcharan Jaggi Kussa is how different protagonists come to the fore and take on aspects of the major events, as they impact on different lives. Santu is cajoled by his mother, a strong character in the early stages, to marry the rape victim Melo. He is reluctant, but when told of the fact she was made pregnant by her assailant, soon agrees for her honour. One starts assuming the child will clash with the father and we will go into a Sikh Muslim affair. That is not what happens. Instead Santu and his "son" fall victim to the anti-naxelite and Akali politics of the late seventies, having seen Punjab split further. Later this family take a back seat and Gurmukh's family come to the fore, at a time when all Kes Dhari Sikhs are seen as the enemy. Like Santu's mother, Amli puts in an important role in the beginning , but fades into the background, as the situations move on, like a fast train to 1984 and Operation Bluestar. Not the politics but the human cost. Throughout Gyani Ji remains a major character uniting all the sub-plots, which are all linked through the evil Mayor as well. Where necessary, Shivcharan Jaggi Kussa is economical with his words, where elsewhere he goes into detail. Whichever method he uses, he evokes clear stark images and moods within the readers mind and heart. The right choice of words, and the heavy use of conversation and colloquial language adds spice to the novel. Beautiful vivid language is used. He really understand the average Punjabi everyman, and the use of words tells us all we need to know about each character, acting as a window to their souls. To say anymore would give too much away. I not only recommend this most excellent Punjabi novel (The best I have read to date), but suggest that all his books should be explored. This author's books must be translated in to Spanish, English, Chinese, Japanese, Hindi and Arabic. The world is missing out on what Punjabi Literature has to offer, and in terms of Novels, he is probably the best.

- Roop Dhillon

The Triveni[1] Speaks

Maut Ki kis se trarafdaari hai,
Aaj hamaari, aur kal tumhaari vaari hai.

(Death favours none. If it's our turn today,
tomorrow, it will be yours.)

It was the evening of 9 November 1984. So much of unexpected had happened. It had pierced the hearts full of compassion for mankind as a whole.

I was smoky outside.

Eeerie silence pervaded the atmosphere.

The streets exuded a stench of human flesh.

The stray dogs dragged the human corpses in the streets. The vulture hovered in the sky. It was very suffocating indeed!

The entreaties of innocent kids had vanished in the elegiac air. The shrieks of humanity were devoured by the heart-rending air.

It was the aftermath of a cataclysm.

What was left behind but a trail of devastation?

The sighs and festering wounds of suffering humanity!

The wails had turned into sobs. A question: Do we belong to this very country? was etched into the minds of victims.

"What makes you so speechless? You have been lip-stitched for the last few days!" The Banyan asked the aged neem which was

---

[1] A trinity of peepal, banyan and neem (margosa) tree

a part of the Triveni grown outside the house of Baba Gurmukh Singh.

"What to say? Had god given me feet....?" the tight-lipped Neem heaved a sigh as if some hurricane had shaken it at the roots.... As a widow sighs at the sight of her only son's dead body.

"............" The hoary Banyan stood drowned in extreme despondence. With its roots firmly stuck in to the cemented platform, it felt itself like the one with shackled feet.

"For so many days I haven't had the touch of Baba Gurmkh Singh's feet and it makes me cry....!" The Neem burst in to tears! The silent tears! Silent but tremulous like mercury!

"How can you....? The Baba is killed by the rascals......" the throat of the peepal standing close by was choked with emotion.

"Disasters have always been the destiny of man but this calamity....?" Neem's heart bled and soul cried as it said this.

"We have seen the worst of times during the century but never did I imagine such a brutality of man on man........"

The old Neem found it hard to contain its sinking heart.

"What war they have won by killing the saintly Baba and Kulbira....?" A torrent of tears was unleashed from its eyes.

A volcano erupted in the bosom.

"O, my God....!" the Banyan too could not help shedding an unabated spate of tears.

This Triveni had braved so many inclemencies of time together- the gales, dust-storms, winter, summer, weal, woe etc.

But such a savagery, high-handedness and earthshaking barbarits had been unprecedented so far. Peepal, Banyan and Neem were literally the standing history of nearly a full century. The invaders came, rampaged and decamped. But this animalism ...? An innocent child and his grandfather..... ? O God.... !! "

Je sakta sakte kau maare ta mann ros na hoiee *(There is nothing to feel aggrieved if the mighty kills the mighty.)*

"Baba and Kulbir a also must have remembered us.... ?" When Peepal touched the suppurating wound, the Neem's heart seemed to have blasted out of its chest. The air too wailed in tremendous grief.

It put its hand on the bursting chest.

"Now who is going to remember us, you fool.... ?"

"The dead never turn up..... !"

"Lots of people came and departed but I don't know what bound us to Baba and Kulbira ... ?"

"It's only the bonds of love, passion and thinking which bind people together.... !"

If Banyan, Peepal and Neem can have a throbbing heart, then why don't we, the humans, have it?"

Are we really human beings?

Aren't we animals?

Aren't we devils?

Are we.... ??

- The earlier wise men used to say : A time will come when very rarely you will find the glow of a lamp- You see, this is how it has all happened... Is there any doubt now?

Thus speaking, the Triveni faded out in darkness- a dreadful darkness....!!

It was a very hot evening. The harvesting of Rabi crop was round the corner. People were girding up their loins for harvesting at a war-plane. Shakkar[2] was being brought generously in all the

---

[2] The addict. N.B. Amli ia s well-known character in almost every village of Punjab. He is known for his wit, outspokenness and skill of repartee.

homes. There was no dearth of pure ghee anywhere. The farm laborers were being engaged. The reaping of crops and its threshing are the occasions no less festive and exuberant in a farmer's family.

"How are you Santu chacha[3].... ?" said Asgher while Santu was going to the ironsmith for getting his sickle serrated.

"I am fine Asghar...."

"Ready for reaping wheat?"

"Absolutely...."

"To which artisan are you going chacha?"

"Waryam....."

"Go ahead then. I am also coming in a short while."

Asghar went on his way.

There was a pretty good gathering of farmers in Waryam's verandah. They were all eager to get the teeth of their respective sickles sharpened. He and his three sons were awfully busy these days.

"Oh, it's too hot today..." said Waryam while wiping aside the beads of perspiration from his forehead. It had come down like a stream on the ground.

"Want anything ... Water etc..." said Nathu amli.[4]

"Oh, yes, bring it yaar."

"Amlia! Now even if the ironsmith asks the jatt[5] to fan him, he will not say no.

"His own interest lies in it now!"

"Of course, otherwise a jatt will not even urinate on the wound of the artisan", Waryam's son remarked..

---

[3] Jatt is the dominant caste-group in villages who are basically agriculturists.

[4] Raw sugar

[5] Younger brother of father.

"If you go for a sheaf of dry chaff from their fields, they will never oblige so easily."

"They are the most gentle ones only during the harvesting season."

"Doestn't matter mistri[6] uncle, it's a matter of need only."

"Now you take the example of Kaadar…," Nathu amli started saying, "If you ask his wife 'How are you bhabi?', she would say, 'I am fine Bhai jaan[7]'. Now if someone should ask her, 'What makes me your Bhaijaan? Hunh… Treat me as your devar[8] if you have to."

Amli's wish to be called devar made everybody laugh.

"And that too a beloved devar!"

It made the laughter more boisterous.

"No, no amlia, yours is no age to become devar now.

Kaadar's remark made amli feel small.

"Reducing his age like this amli has every chance to retreat in to the womb of his mother," said Waryam and made all have a hearty laugh.

"Kaadra today is the day that even your Bashiran will come to cook food for the mistri uncle if he wishes this, "said amli as if by way of face-saving only.

"……" Kaadar remained silent.

"You talk of cooking food? If uncle asks her to wash his kachhehra[9], she will obey and massage his legs as well… "

"The uncle doesn't wear any kachhehra at all. He wears only a small underwear."

---

[6] Artisan

[7] A respectful address for elder brother.

[8] Brother-in-law

[9] A long underwear.

"What to speak of washing kachhehras, if uncle asks her to live with him till the start of Rabi harvesting, she won't say 'no' to him."

The ironsmith chuckled at this jabber.

He felt himself young in the company of village youngsters. His verandah was lucky enough to have under the same roof men of different faiths. Hindus, Sikhs, Muslims etc. all sat together like a well-knit family there.

"We may or may not find time during the harvest season, so chacha let's enjoy a peg or two today," Asghar proposed to Santu while putting aside a bundle of sickles.

"That we can do but I'm afraid your abba[10] will scold me for spoiling his son," Santu said

"How can you spoil the already spoilt?"

"Who ever taught the peacock to dance?"

"They say India is going to be freed?" Someone came out with this news.

"This we have been hearing since long. What's new in it?"

"Come what may, we are to reap wheat after all. Nobody is going to make us ministers," amli couldn't help commenting on such an important issue.

"Only those with pot- bellies will become ministers, not we," said another.

"The firangi[11] is not going to leave here so easily. He will definitely play some mischief."

"You fool, has anybody given up an empire."

"Had traitors like Dhyan Singh Dogra not betrayed. The firangi would never dared to look towards this side."

---

[10] Father

[11] A sect of baptized sikhs

"It's only the insiders who stab in the back."

"Whaeguruji Ka Khalsa- Waheguru ji Ki fateh," Giani Pooran Singh came with his traditional greeting to the gossipers. The greeting was duly reciprocated by all who sat there.

"Come on Baba ji, Welcome!"

"Thank you…. "

"Giani Ji, anything new? Waryam, the ironsmith asked. Giani Pooran Singh was a devout Sikh. Being educated and sensible he had a good flair for politics.

"The circumstances donot appear very good to me." the Giani nodded his head in frustration.

"……. " Everybody looked at the Giani's face in utter silence and with a sign of interrogation writ large on their own faces.

"Still Giani Ji?" The amli broke the silence.

"They say India will split and Pakistan will emerge.?" Someone expressed his curiosity.

"We can't say anything, but definitely it's in the air," the Giani replied.

"People are not in favour of separation even a bit, but the leaders-just for their own lust for power can draw a dividing line any time."

They felt stunned to hear this.

"Now they will separate borthers from brothers. A throbbing heart will be divided in twain. Above, the sky is father to all and earth is mother. Will they divide the sky and earth also? What kind of freedom will it be, Oh God! Pieces of mother earth? Division of sky? Murder of passions? Destruction of love and other sentiments? Decimation of the future of communities?"

The hilarious atmosphere prevailing just hithertofore, was now charged with a silence of the graveyard.

"But Giani Ji, what about the properties here and that side of the border?" Jaagar was worried about property more than life.

"I think they will allot land-holdings this side to those coming from there and that side to those migrating from here. Definitely, some arrangement of this kind will be made." The Giani just visualized the whole thing.

"I fail to understand one thing," the mistri said, "Why are they out to displace the well-settled people?"

"Of course, let them get freedom. Who stops them?"

"This is a well-contemplated move of the British. He doesn't want to take risk of leaving such a vast country as it. Both the followers of Jinnah and Nehru have their eye on the seats of power ministries. And the English rules will partition the country by taking advantage of this situation. He is taking separate meeting with Hindu and Muslim politicians everyday. These whites are not only cunning, they will prove also fatal for us. On one side they are provoking the Nehru group that so long as the shrewd Jinnah is there, there is no chance of Nehru's becoming the prime-minister while on the other the Jinnahites are being told that they can never rule in a Hindu-majority country. The seeds of fear and hatred are being sown in the hearts on both the sides. So in the prevailing situation. I feel, Pakistan must come in to existence.

"......." A deadly silence gripped all the listeners. It was a mysterious and horrendous narration.

"But Giani Ji, how will the partition benefit the English? Waryam, the ironsmith asked with his mouth agape.

"Are you really a fool?" The well-informed Giani laughed at his naivety.

"Nobody dares cast an evil eye on a well-integrated family where even two well-built brothers live together. If the brothers separate from each other and keep quarreling every other day, any Santa, Banta would arise to become a mediator between them. Similar is the case with British. They want India to split so that both India and Pakistan should keep fighting with each other and have no time to think about their two centuries long period of slavery."

" ....."

"And you see the cunningness of the English. They allure anybody who produces twelve children with a piece of cultivable land. Why? The one who fathers twelve children will, no doubt, get land but he will become so much engaged with rearing them that he can never dream of freedom. Moreover, they were not to allot this land from their own property. It was already ours. The only aim was to make the life of common man so complicated that he should not think of freedom. So it's not only one policy but so many of this kind. They are so mean that they will never let anybody know their actual intentions. Divide and Rule is their well known strategy. What to speak of common man, even the politicians fail to understand them. And even if some of them do understand they prefer to keep silent. You see, before leaving, they will give us such an injury that will become a never-healing boil in due course of time. And the people will keep groaning with its pain; the Giani harangued.

" ...." Some of the listeners could understand him while the others couldn't make any head or tail of it.

"But Giani Ji."

"Yes?"

"What will be the areas of India and Pakistan? Any borders?"

"As per the news- so far as I think-Delhi will be the capital of India while Lahore will be that of Pakistan. This side of Wagah will be Pakishatn and that side of the border will be India.

"And what will be the fate of Hindus and Sikhs living here and Mussalmans living there?"

"Ruin, what else....?"

"This is gross injustice, yaar."

"Feel lucky if it stops at displacement only," the Giani said and scared everybody.

"What worse can there be?" the frightened mistri had in a way voiced some inner shriek. His heart seemed to be sinking to hear about the possibility of such un-thought of incidents.

"Bloodshed!"

"Bloodshed…?" Everybody felt benumbed at this single word.

"Bloodshed-I mean, a fratricidal war."

"But why?" All of them were flabbergasted.

"The English must engineer Hindu-Muslim riots for sowing the seeds of hatred.

Nobody had believed the wise man's words. They were wonderstruck to think as to why would both the communities living hand in glove for centuries, rise up in arms against each other.

Asghar Mohammad and Santu were sharing a drink at night. The bottle of country liquor lying before them looked ready to explode like a bomb. But they were not talking much to each other, as if the deaf and dumb were sitting for a booze. More than the draughts of liquor, the words of Giani Pooran Singh had a bigger sway on their minds. One and only the one question was hitting their heads like a sledge- hammer: Why shall the people living together since decades, sharing weal and woe of each other, fight with each other? Where is the scope for a bloodbath? How will those-who treat the children, daughters and sisters of each other as their own-attack each other?

Asghar recalled well how the whole Sikh community had stood united against Geja, the Nihang1 who had tried to usurp the plot owned by the poor man Nizamudin.

"Geja, don't treat Nizamudin as poor and helpless. We'll teach you such a lesson as you will remember throughout your life if you even looked at his plot," Baba Nidhan Singh had challenged the Nihang openly in the village sath[12].

"You being Sikhs will stand by this mean pauper?" The seven-feet statured Geja's voice had echoed in the sath like the sound of a trumpet.

"We are the voice of the poor first and Sikh afterwards. So clear your mind of this communal virus and vacate the plot like a gentleman, otherwise don't say we had not warned you earlier," the Giani said.

"Baba, it will make us enemies for generations", the Nihang tried to threaten the Baba in a covert manner.

"Whom are you trying to scare, you Nihang. Just one blow on your temples will keep reminding you of your folly throughout life.

"........"

"Baba even doesn't know even the impact of blow at a particular part of the body," someone said.

"You threaten me? I am the beloved Singh[13] of Kalgidhar[14]."

"Oi you! And Kalgidhar's Singh? Why invite the punishment of sins on yourself by saying so? The Kalgidhar had sacrificed his whole family for the oppressed. And you… you are out to exploit a poor man? Get lost and don't say anything more…." The Baba trembled in rage as he said this.

"Go then, do whatever you like. I will possess the plot right tomorrow," the Nihang said as a final threat.

"Okay then. I will see to it how you grab the poor man's plot. Tomorrow, either you or I will survive. One of us is sure to die. So come prepared if you are really the son of your father."

---

[12] Assembly point for villagers, also called 'chaupal'

[13] Sikh, lion as brave as. (A common belief that a baptized sikh becomes as brave as a lion.)

[14] One who wears a Kalghi i.e. plume. Here it means the tenth Sikh Master Guru Gobind Singh

The supporters of both sides pacified them with their intervention.

The Baba came home infuriated like a wounded lion.

"Oi Gurmukha!" the Baba called his adolescent son in a thunderous voice.

"Yes Bapu?" The only one and very docile boy responded immediately.

"Come, take mem charpoy to the plot of Nizamuddin."

Gurumukh Singh took away his father's charpoy.

"What is the matter… ?" Partap Kaur, the Baba's wife asked. She had never seen her husband in this mood.

"What to tell you Partapi, the people won't let the poor live in peace."

"Still, what's the matter?"

"In fact, Geja Nihang is hell bent on grabbing Nizamuddin's plot. Morever, he threatens also. Nizamuddin is a poorman. He doesn't say anything and supplicates with folded hands before him. This is what encouraged the Nihang still more. Had it been some equal, he would have knocked him down by now and beaten him to blue…", said the Baba while sharpening his spear simultaneously.

"What a worm-eaten brain, he is!" Partapi exclaimed in disgust.

"You send my food there only. So long as Nizamuddin doesn't build a boundary-wall round his plot and takes possession of it, I will remain there."

"Won't you take milk?"

"Send it also alongwith the food." And the Baba left as smoothly and hastily as railway engine.

From that day onwards the Baba laid his charpoy in Nizamuddin's plot and remained there till its possession was taken by him. But the Nihang never turned up. He was well familiar with the Baba's nature. The Baba was very aggressive when an occasion arose but was extremely gentle otherwise.

"Pour another peg now! What are you thinking off so seriously..?" Santu said to Asghar who was engrossed in some thoughts deep down the memory lane.

In such a somber atmosphere, they finished the bottle. Razia came with the bundle of chapattis.

Santu and Asghar mealed together but their spirit seemed to have remained enmeshed somewhere in the nitty-gritty of Indo-Pakistan partition. Nobody was ready to believe it to become a reality. But everybody was greatly worried over the issue and calming his mind with a sham consolation. Hindu, Sikh and Muslim industrialists had started their deals with their respective governments. The Hindus and Sikhs had identified their places in India while the Muslims had done so in Pakistan.

This partition would descend as a bolt from the blue for the poor only who were to receive almost nothing by way of compensation. The capitalists or industrialists had nothing to lose as they were to get an equal share on both sides of the border. Many Hindus, Sikhs and Muslims had even decided to exchange their business.

The harvesting of wheat had started.

Those who had sown later, came to the help of those who sowed it earlier. The people had not as yet been compartmentalized as Hindus, Sikhs and Muslims. They were still human beings. The fraternal bonds were intact so far.

The harvesting and threshing of Rabi concluded very amicably.

The people had sown kharif now.

Freed from the fields, the people got busy with other things like arrangement of marriages etc. Everybody had his own liabilities. The people of all the communities were perfectly helpful to each other.

The news about India and Pakistan were assuming a strange shape everyday.

Intermittent news about partition had become a routine affair now. But people still didn't pay much attention to them.

The Hindus and Mussalmans had now started playing their fiddle more openly and mud-slinging on each other started in a big way. The shrewd English man was adding fuel to the fire very rapidly. His main objective was to split the well- integrated India in to India and Pakistan. The 'Divide and Rule' Policy was assuming formidable proportions day in and day out.

At last the communal groups started raising slogans of Zindabad (Long Live) and Murdabad (Down with). While the Hindus and Sikhs trumpeted the Pakistan Murdabad slogan, it was Hindustan Murdabad with the Mussalmans.

The association of the men of each religion with the faction of their own country was quite natural at a pychlological level. Nobody could defy this urge. The virus of communalism was such that even the old men sharing hubble-bubble in the sath would squabble with each other. Those living amicably for centuries together would exercise restraint of course but the communal conflagration was taking the innocent people in to its bear-hug everyday.

"Don't know what has gone wrong with the people living at peace with each other", Chetu, the old sire would say in utter disgust with the diabolic politics.

"They are prone to bark from a higher pedestal but you the innocent people, please you don't be foolish."

"They have to invent any one or the other problem, but you are the ones to see reason and eat the daily bread with the sweat of your brow."

"There is no running away Baba. When you daily hear a new mischief, something must happen after all."

"The communal virus is very contagious my friend."

"They will enter the parliament-house in new Delhi. Only the common man will come at the receiving end."

"Baba to whom will you try to persuade now? It has become a common malaise now."

"My child you see they will make the brother fight against brother by encouraging the virus of communalism."

The month of Sawan was at its full swing. Riots had started here and there. The people condemned as they heard it and the grey-bearded senior citizens would curse them without knowing much about the political scenario."

"Fie with you and your politics.?"

"Hell with such a politics!"

The advent of Bhadon the desi month was at it peak and the English month August was very ominous. A cataclysm came from all the sides. The fanatic Hindus in India and Mussalmans in Pakistan started molesting the sisters and daughters of each other.

The dirty politics had created a wedge between the people who had been living at peace for centuries together.

If some miscreant rumoured in Pakistan that a trainload of Muslim corpses had come from India then the Hindus and Sikhs had to face a bloodbath in Pakistan.

The neighbors became aliens to each other overnight.

Thousand of women were abducted.

The houses were plundered

The molestation of daughters and sisters had crossed all bounds. Men like Chiraghdin who had never seen a woman in life, seduced at least three-four women in a single night. The paupers like Gujjar Khan became millionaires overnight with the looted booty.

Nizamuddin hacked Geja. the Nihang with the support of local Mussalmans. Gurmukh Singh's father Baba Nidhan Singh was killed while rescuing the honour of a Hindu damsel. Santu's Pala was burnt alive by the sons of Kallho, the midwife due to just negligible animosity. They had packed him in a wooden box and the set it ablaze. Santi had swooned at the right of barbarity.

What to say more, a whirlwind of communalism came and razed to dust the happily living people. The homes were destroyed along with the houses.

At this junction, Kaadar helped Santu a lot. He was sheltered for two days from the fury of the maniacs after Pala's death.

Hazoor Singh, Gurmukh, Santu, Baghtu, amli, Thamman, Jaagar, Santi and Har Kaur had sought refuge in Asghar's house only. They were getting whatever food could possibly be given to them.

The streets and fields of the village had become deserted and death seemed to be serenading at every roof or parapet. The entire families had been eliminated. The robbers rather than police or army, were stalking the streets.

Gurmukh Singh's aged mother too had died in grief for her husband Baba Nidhan Singh. She was cremated in broad daylight in Asghar's out-house. One more mattress of grief was laid.

"Chacha, may I say one thing?" a grief-stricken Asghar asked Santu.

"Yes" Santu seemed to have spoken from the depth of a well.

"I don't feel like saying, but…." Asghar found if hard to speak.

"No, no you just say what you have to. You have sheltered us in bad times. I don't know whether I will be able to reciprocate you any time or not." Santu became emotional as he said this.

"Don't feel bad chacha, only man can help man."

"They were also men Asghar who ruined so many homes." Thamman hinted at the hooligans.

"They are the sons of some bitch Chacha".

"…." A silence permeated the atmosphere.

"You were about to say something?"

"Chacha, I was asking when will this animalism end? Everyday radio broadcasts appealed that Hindus and Sikhs should leave Pakistan and come to India. If the looters come here, it will be very difficult to save you. Please don't misunderstand Chacha. I have no objection. From my side you are welcome here as long as you like. But if you are ready to leave, I and Kaadar can help you cross the border at night. There you have your own government. Here you have only risk on your life… but please don't take it otherwise Chacha," Asghar said and started weeping bitterly.

"Asghar is right."

Everybody felt sad at this sorry state of affairs.

They were ready to flee the place where they had spent life together. It was as if their native land was throwing them out. The blood had turned white. The nails had left the flesh. All were sad and a sense of abject helplessness was gnawing at their innards.

"If the situation ever gets back to normalcy, you must come back. Asghar will always remain your son."

Santu took him in his embrace.

"Living, you stand every chance to meet again." Asghar was crying.

"What life has this government left here? All the souls have burnt alive, you Saleems's abba. Razia was very sad at heart.

"What will they gain from Pakistan or Hindustan? So much loss of life is already done."

"You can't understand this politics my child."

"Hell with such politics,Chacha."

"They don't feel a thorn-prick even if the remaining world also dies."

Santu's wife Santi was very much crestfallen. She called her son Pala aloud time and again. Har Kaur consoled her. Santi would call Mussalmans as dogs and hurl invectives on them. Har kaur would silence her by gagging her mouth with her hand. Sometimes she would bite Har kaur's hand and at times she started lamentations. Everybody felt panicked at the very thought of the vandalists.

But Santu had borne the death of his son with great fortitude.

"Let's leave right tonight."

"Yes, we'll see what happens."

"One has to die after all, sooner or later."

"Then why die indoors like lepers?"

"Furthermore we are here like a burden on Asghar," Gurmukh had said after a long silence."

"Brother Gurmukh, you are no burden at all on me. I am scared of the situation only; Asghar looked ahead of his times.

Kaadar, Bashiran and Razia sat scratching the earth Santi had fallen asleep somehow.

Har Kaur was sitting at her head side.

Night had descended with a pall of darkness. All of them loaded their luggage on bullock-carts. In another cart, a sheet was spread for Santi to sleep on.

Santi lay motionless.

While loading the luggage nobody talked to each other as if they were deaf and dumb; as if their tongues had been cut; as if they had forgotten speaking; as if they were the denizens of a desolate island-some aborigines.

They partook the food prepared by Razia. She had packed jumbo-sized praunthas alongwith gur2, onions and mango-pickle.

"Ok, remember Waheguru now and start." Santu called out to his comrades.

"......" In a way, all had a shudder down their spine. Love for the native soil had welled up in the form of tears in his eyes. Everybody was trying to conceal his tears.

"Come on Santi, come!" Santu said to his wife with a great self-restraint on his part.

"Where?" Santi asked in state of delirium.

"Wherever God may take us."

"And Pala will stay back here?"

"....." Nobody spoke a word

"Pala's Bapu-here his soul will wander restless without us. I won't go anywhere."

"This is how it was destined Santi. We are bound to go where God would take us for a loaf of bread. Come, get up. Don't be a fool Trust in His will."

"I won't go without Pala." Santi, in a way. announced her decision. All were standing helpess.

"You get up and come along for God's sake. On one hand the circumstances conspire against us and on the other she is out to harass us." A vexed Santu said.

"You just come for once and show me your face, O Pala...." Santi's wails rent the hearts of all.

"I kept raising you with milk and butter for these wolves, O my beloved Pala...

"........"

"Your mother's heart is burnt to coals, my son."

"Now have patience Santi. Trust in God." Har Kaur tried to console her.

Bashiran gave her water to drink.

Razia stood weeping there.

As the carts set out on their journey, Santi fainted. All were worried. Cold water was sprinkled on her face. It was a fit of catalepsy which was undone by opening her locked jaw with the help of spoon.

Santi regained some conciousness.

"Santi the path is long. We can reach somewhere only if you contain yourself. Steel your heart with Guru's blessings. Nobody can stand against His will." Har Kaur entreated in a way.

"How can I steel my heart? God had given me only one child... that too these Muslas have finished. May God destroy you O Muslas..."

"This bitch will get all of us killed today." Santu got annoyed.

"Keep peace Santu. All mothers' hearts are like that." Thamman combed his dense beard with his fingers as he said this.

Razia brought the cauldron of tea.

Everyone had tea.

After tea Kaddar placed before them weapons of all kinds including swords, axes, choppers and a bludgeon.

"These will be of use in the way, Chacha."

"Leave them right up to the border. If government has shut eyes on its responsibilities, at least we are the same." Razia directed Asghar while handing him an old pistol.

"Don't worry Razia, we'll return only after sending them across the border."

They all blessed Razia and Bashiran by placing elderly hand on their heads.

The carts started moving.

All had wept bitterly at this heavy moment.

"Chacha if the situation comes back to normal, please do come back-and don't forget us." Razia had said to all amidst tears.

"We too are not going to be comfortable without you beti, but there seems to be no chance of improvement in the situation."

"Who knows the will of God, Chacha? These bloody swines of government are not gods after all."

"Razia, now you go back," Kaadar told Razia and Bashiran who were coming along.

The carts stopped for a while and everybody cried himself or herself out.

Razia and Bashiran returned weeping.

The carts kept moving at a steady pace throughout the night.

Nothing untoward had happened.

Kaadar and Asghar had at time piloted and at times escorted the caravan with arms. All moved on with bated breaths. But Santi had been sleeping and waking in between. She was suffering from a strange restlessness.

At dawn they were attacked from one side.

Santu and others also became cautious, well-armed as they were and the clash ensued for ten-fifteen minutes.

Gurmukh's arm received a gash in this assault. A lance had torn flesh from one of his biceps. Asghar opened fire in self defence. It made the assailants run amock. The leader of the group had received many pellets. So before the second fire would come, they ran helter-skelter.

"Are you Okay?" Hazoor Singh caught Gurmukh Singh from his arm and bandaged the wound by tearing away a piece of cloth from his turban.

But the blood was still oozing out of the dressing.

'No I am all right Taya[15]." Gurmukh had controlled his pain somehow.

"Gurumukh, just listen to me," Kaadar said.

"Yes?"

"Just come aside-let me urinate on the wound."

"Nothing to worry. The wound will not grow ripe with urine."

"Urine is a medicine for the wound, dear."

"Yes, come on, don't be shy."

They moved aside. The jet of urine worked like spirit, gave a very excruciating burning sensation and made Gurmukh groan in pain.

"It's the turn of destiny Gurmukha! Otherwise what was the problem? Anyway whatever God does is right. We have to bow before His will.

As the sun darted its first ray on earth, they pacified their hunger by eating praunthas.

They drank water from the stream flowing nearby. It filled them with a sort of confidence.

---

[15] Father's elder brother

"Chacha, I and Kaadar will keep watch. You have a nap upto noon. Let the animals also have rest," said Asghar.

"Let's have them drink water first. The poor cattle can't speak out their thirst to us."

All of them made their respective bullocks drink water. Some quantity of hay was also served to them.

They laid their sacks under a banyan tree on the bank of the stream and due to night-long fatigue had a sound sleep there.

Some others, also dislodged like others kept coming and stopping near the banyan tree.

By noon it became a pretty big caravan under the tree. Due to a common bond of suffering, they picked up courage. Now they had started feeling fearless in the company of each other.

They shared their tales of woe and cursed the governments of India and Pakistan Someone had lost his son and someother his father. Someone's daughter had been abducted. So much so that the parents themselves had pushed their passionately brought up young daughters into the well to save them from the molestation at the hands of Mussalmans. Due to the lust of a handful of megalomaniacs, the humanity had fallen in to the abysses of such savagery. The people on both sides of the border had been uprooted.

Next evening, the caravan reached Wahga border. Santu and others like him were in a fix out of an unknown fright.

The other day, this border had witnessed a number of gory skirmishes.

The caravans from both sides were marching to their respective new destinations. It was a very strange situation and mysterious atmosphere. Everybody was in the grip of a pitiable mental conflict. Heart-rending incidents were taking place en route.

"Well Chacha, we'll take leave now," said Asghar. "Right Asghar, we can't pay back what you have done for us."

"What are you talking Chacha," Asghar embraced Santu and burst into tears.

It was a very gloomy atmosphere.

"Chacha you must keep writing to us as and when you have a foothold there," Kaadar said.

"Yes, of course. Why not?"

"Now you push off. Don't waste time," said Thamman.

"Gurmukha you must get your arm dressed in the camp. It is an iron-injury.. may get worse."

"Yes, I will."

"Take care of Santi Chachi

"All right."

With heavy hearts Kaadar and Asghar went back. Those who lived together day and night were parting away perhaps for ever. The monster of riots had killed the man in Man. The rulers of the time had fulfilled their will but the common man had put up with all this affront to humanity as the will of Providence.

Traveling for a full night and half a day, they had reached Ferozepur camp. The camp too had turned in to a hub of sobs and shrieks. The people moved about with unfathomable agony buried in their bosoms. It was a mind-boggling chaos. Not men but living corpses seemed to be moving about.

They parked their bullock-carts on one side of the camp in a desolate place. The oxen had a sigh of relief. All were badly fatigued. They fell asleep inspite of thirst and hunger biting at the entrails.

At midnight the screams of someone shook the whole camp out of slumber. Startled, all of them got up. They were awfully sedated with sleep.

The subdued cries rose once again. It was a young girl.

When Santu and some others rushed to the site, they found the young girl tied to the cart with ropes. Close by her parents sat with downcast eyes. The girl was looking with a blank glance.

"Mother, what ails the girl?" Thamman asked.

"......." The mother was sitting with her gaze fixed on the ground

"Mayee[16], why have you tied the girl?" Hazoor Singh asked sternly.

"......" The father too looked petrified. Quite cold.

"But why don't you tell anything?" When Hazoor Singh lost his patience, the mother's pent up anger broke all barriers of silence and said.

"These muslas[17] have ruined her. Eleven men gang-raped her. This is what has sent her out of her mind. That's why we have tied her. If we untie her she rushes at once to jump into the well. But if we tie her she starts screaming aloud. Do you

have any solution to the problem? Can you....?" The old woman was getting more and more aggressive.

It silenced everybody including Hazoor Singh. Everybody felt duped.

"Now what to do but face-saving, O God!" the despondent mother said and started weeping.

Hazoor Singh was dumbfounded as he looked at the girl in the pale lantern light. Seventeen-eighteen years girl was bitten all over by 'human' teeth. As if some wolves had bruised her with claws.

The girl was actually out of her mind. Seeing Hazoor Singh so near to her she started making entreaties. "Taya, save me for God's sake. I will cook your food, serve your cattle and massage your legs. But please save me. See how they have maltreated me." Saying this, the girl uncovered her breasts before all. Hazoor

[16] Mother

[17] A contemptuous word for mussalmans.

Singh withdrew the lantern from the scene. He was moved at heart to see this brutality. His soul was crushed under the guilt for which the brutes of her daughter. The father heart was split in twain masquerading as men were responsible. The girl's mother got up and covered the breasts with agony He had failed to resist eleven men.

"You come from?" Hazoor Singh asked.

"Bahawalpur."

Hazoor Singh became silent. He didn't want to sprinkle chillies on their gaping wounds by saying something.

"Be strong gentleman. Getting disheartened like this will not do any good. Tomorrow we shall take the girl to the camp doctor."

"......" He was speechless.

"Alone?"

"Yes.... "

"Any other man or woman from the family?"

"I had two sons. They have been hacked to death by the Mussalmans. She is the younger girl and you have already seen her condition. I had a younger brother also. There is no word about his family also. Can't say whether someone has survived or not..." He again hid his head between his knees.

"These are the ways of God, my dear," said Thamman looking at Hazoor Singh.

The girl had after all gone asleep due to the weariness caused by too much of wailing. The mother covered her with a khes.

In utter frustration, all went to their beds.

The cries of someone disturbed the sleep of everybody early in the morning. The were sleeping in the open like gypsies.

They all rushed to the site at once and what they saw swept them off their feet. They felt the earth slipping from under their feet. The rape-victim girl's father had hanged himself from a branch of sheesham tree.

His wife was weeping bitterly.

The girl witnessed the scene silently.

The able-bodied youngsters brought the dead body down to the earth

The whole atmosphere was charged with grief.

The dead body was bathed in a formal way and then cremated after garnering the fuel wood.

All of the victims of partition stood speechless as if petrified. As if everybody had lost someone of his kins. The lamentations of the deceased's wife pierced the hearts of all. First, two young sons and now her husband had also deserted her. Furthermore, she had acquired the extra liability of a demented daughter. Her life had become desolate.

They had hardly returned after cremation when an old man reached there in a very pitiable condition. He called out, "Oye Babloo" time and again.

"What's the matter grand sire. You seem very puzzled?" Hazoor Singh asked.

"What to tell you dear, I have lost may two little grandsons…" The old man burst in to sobs. His snow-white beard was already drenched with tears.

"Where did you lose them?"

"Don't know. They had come to drink water but didn't turn up."

"When did they come?"

"About an hour or so."

"Searched on camp hand pump?"

"I have covered about three miles in search of them but God knows where they are and how?" The old man again started shedding the tears of helplessness.

It touched the hearts of everybody present there.

"Please don't lose heart, you grand old man. We'll search for the boys."

The search for the Baba's grandsons started all over the camp.

The old man was bewildered with grief.

The words "Oye Babloo" now started escaping his lips in an intermittent manner. They combed the whole camp area but failed to trace the children.

The old man beat his thighs in desperation and sat on the ground. Men like Thamman Singh supported him and made him drink water from the nearby stream.

Search for the children started again.

At last at the sunset hour they found the children from a well. Sitting near an old man, the boys rushed to cling to their grandfather.

The impassioned grandfather started kissing the mouths of the children.

"Where had you gone, O my sweet toys?" The Baba again started crying, "I left nowhere unsearched to find you." He said and picked both of them in his lap.

"They were running, crying when I caught them. I gave them the temptation of gur and sugarcanes and made them sit hear. I was afraid lest the Mussalmans should catch them. These Turks are so ruthless that they don't even spare the children while killing."

"These muslas are a very butcher kind of a community." said Thamman.

"You fool, if someone casts an evil eye on the daughters of our Mama[18] or Chacha, we feel like killing him and they the bastards marry their real cousins saying "We don't marry outside our community."

"I have also heard that if they marry outside their community, they are thrown out of it."

"What a tradition!"

"The sister of Chiraghdin of our village was married to Humayun and Humanyun's Sister was married to Chiraghdin," said Hazoor Singh.

"Really…?" The Baba who had protected the children responded with astonishment.

"And one day it so happened that Chiraghdin went to see his sister Saina. When he reached there he found Humayun beating Saina. He immediately turned back on his feet and started thrashing his wife Sheekan.

"You bloody dog, why are you beating me for nothing?" she asked.

"He was beating Saina and I will beat you," he replied curtly.

"Then?"

"What then, the neighbors rescued her with great effort.

Everybody laughed but not heartily.

Early in the morning they turned up in the camp.

The old man had picked both his grandsons in his lap.

"I have brought them alive by crossing over the deadbodies of their father and Chachas. Now this is the only capital of their grandparents."

"And their mother?"

---

[18] Mother's brother.

"She had been killed by the devils on the very first day. The same day she was cremated. Similarly their father and chachas were also killed the day we had set out. They also robbed us of whatever we had leaving us to see this day. While going they said, "Say our salaam to Gandhi and Nehru.""

The crestfallen grandmother, in a way, blossomed at the sight of her grandsons. She took them into her arms and started weeping. Her love for them started streaming out of her eyes.

Sobs and sighs had become the daily routine of life now.

Santi too would run out of her house at midnight calling aloud her butchered son Pala. Santu and Gurmukh would control her with great difficulty. She tried her best to pluck herself free of their hold but then fell helpless on the ground.

Doctor would come and give some medicine.

With the sedative effect of medicine she would keep lying motionless in the bed and look towards the sky with blank eyes. The tears would flow silently out of her eyes and drop on her ears. The pangs of separation from her son would always sit heavy on her heart. Her only son Pala remained clinging to her chest in her wild fantasies. She could not have a nap throughout the whole night. Whenever her eyelids closed with sleep she would wake up all of a sudden with a mumble.

"She will have to be chained," Santu would say. He was also in grief over the death of his son but he had somehow steeled his heart. He was bearing this shock with great humility and fortitude. Har Kaur would console them time and again.

Next morning, Hazoor Singh, Thamman, Santu and Gurmukh went to the mother of rape-victim girl.

"What's the name of the girl, sister?" Hazoor singh asked.

"Name is Gurmel Kaur but she is called melo by one and all."

"What is your name?"

"Bachint Kaur."

"Bachint Kaur, let's take the girl to the camp-doctor."

"What will the doctor do? Only it will add to her misery. I don't see any hope of her recovery." Bachint Kaur was very much heart-broken.

"But we must do our best and bow to the will of God," Hazoor Singh tired to console her.

"Let God take us also to His abode. I can't see her condition."

"Don't be foolish. Send her with us," said Thamman.

Bachint Kaur took along the girl and walked with them. The girl was walking alongside and looking frightened with wide open eyes.

"Bebe[19], they've come.", saying so, she ran towards the fields with all her force.

Her shrieks had created a commotion.

"Catch her, someone of you! Let her not jump in to the well!" Bachint Kaur raised an alarm for help.

When the camp boys ran to catch her, she sat down then and there hiding her bitten breasts from them.

"Don't kill me please. I will cook your food, clean your house. But please have mercy on me. And don't touch me here. It pains a lot," saying this she uncovered her scratched, bitten bruised breasts before them.

"Get up bady-get up. We are your brothers come, let's go to the doctor," said Gurmukh with a bleeding heart.

Whether she understood anything or not but looking at them with blank frightened eyes, she started walking with them.

They reached the camp doctor.

Hazoor Singh narrated the whole story and the doctor listened with rapt attention.

---

[19] A popular address for mother in rural Punjab.

"Within a day or two, all the refugees are going to be allotted some place. So she should be treated at wherever her family is rehabilitated. It's not a matter of days. It may take months also."

"........" All were listening with bated breath.

"First of all, along with treatment she needs a pleasant atmosphere also. So far as I feel, she cannot have that environment in the camp here. Wherever the family settles, she should be taken to the local temple or Gurdwara. It will provide her a spiritual strength. I give you the medicine; give it to her when she starts weeping and screaming."

"Doctor Sahb, when will the allotment be made?" asked Thamman.

"It won't take much time now. Orders are expected within a day or two.

"....."

"The properties of Mussalmans migrated from this side are being assessed. I hope, allotment will begin within this week."

"What will be the basis of allotment, Sir?" Thamman had not understood anything.

"Don't know. But the in charge for the same has been appointed. The allotment letters will reach him through Rehabilitation Committee. The landed property in Pakistan will be recorded and allotment will be made on the basis of this record only. But this incharge is a very hard nut to crack. He is very jealous of Punjabis in particular."

"What wrong have Punjabis done to him?

"Nothing. Simply, some people are made like that."

They came back with medicine.

This new problem had preoccupied their minds.

"Oye Gurmukha....!" Baghtu amli came running from afar.

They all looked at once towards him.

"There's a good news." He was going out of his breath.

"What?" They fixed their eyes on him.

"Giani Pooran Singh has also reached the camp," the amli said and pleased everybody.

"Its he all right?"

"Where is he?"

"Any injuries etc.?"

Many suchlike questions surfaced at once.

"He is perfectly okay. You go and meet yourself."

They left the girl on the spot and rushed towards Giani Pooran singh. Some unknown joy had energized them. The educated Giani always used to help them as and when an occasion arose.

"Waheguru ji ka Khalsa, Waheguru ji Ki Fateh," The Giani greeted and embraced everybody. One of his arms was bandaged and injured forehead was also dressed.

"How are you Giani Ji?" The tender-aged Gurmukh's eyes were filled with tears as he saw the learned man in such a condition. After the death of Bapu Nidhan Singh, he saw a great mentor and patron in him. Although the Giani was in the age of being his chacha, yet like others, he also addressed him as 'Giani Ji'

"I have nothing against God now. After I have found you my own village folks," the Giani said and folded his hands skywards.

"Faced any trouble?" Hazoor Singh asked.

"There's nowhere without trouble these days, Hazoor Singh. Here, Lahore-side looks comparatively peaceful but there towards Toba Tek Singh. It was a spectacle of dead bodies everywhere. You see, the mothers couldn't recognize their sons. I say, disaster everywhere. Not one, thousands of families have left their well-equipped houses and come over to this side just for life."

"What about you?"

"We also loaded a little bit of luggage on bullock-carts and set out for the new destination."

"How did you get these injuries?" Gurmukh asked.

"We were attacked near Behbalpur."

"Then?"

"What then? We also pulled swords out of the sheaths and made the Turks run helter skelter. They had thought that in fright we would give-them all with folded hands. And you know, who can defeat a Guru's Singh? One of them laid his hand on the waist-cloth."

"Then?"

"In fact, I had silver-rupees fastened to my waist. "Why do you invite death? Give these rupees to me yourself" he said. I felt the pulse of time and put forward the cloth containing the rupees. As he stretched his arm to take it, I severed his arm from the bicep with a single stroke of sword. Frightened and crying aloud he took to his heels. It emboldened my comrades also. We got injuries but with God's grace there was no loss of life. Then we kept marching with the recitation of Chaupai Sahib (a part of Gurbani) on our lips and stopped here only.

"And what about injuries?"

"Nothing! Only an axe cut on the arm and a stick injury on the forehead.

"Only the neck of the jatt should be intact he never dies with such injuries. "Thamman said.

"These muslas have forgotten God altogether. They spare not even the small children."

"No no! It's not like this," the Giani interrupted.

"All are not alike. There are very nice people also. You yourself have seen how many of them have rescued Hindus and Sikhs risking their own life. Those who murder and plunder are goondas and looters only. Nobody asks them in suchlike situations. Rather they are on the look out for such chances so as to lift booties. They rejoice over these like blood-lettings as one enjoys a wedding."

"This is also right," Thamman agreed to the Giani.

"Moreover Indian goons too are second to none. They too have done the same. This is, in fact, a battle between good and bad. It has always been there in the world and will go on like this."

".........." All listened to Giani Pooran Singh very attentively.

"Guru Nanak had not described Babar as a tyrant. When his forces indulged in blind killings, he had complained to God saying, 'Eti maar paiee kurlaane tain ki dard na aaya?' (*O God didn't your heart melt at such a savagery?*) When Babar's troops went on a rampage and killing spree, the Master said this also, 'Paap Ki Janjj lei Kablon dhaaya, jorin mange daan ve Laalo. Sarm dharm doi chhup khaloi, Kood phirei pardhaan ve Lalo.' He (Babear) has come from Kabul with a band of sinners and is extorting money from the public. Shame and religion, both have hidden themselves somewhere and Falsehood rules the roost everywhere] Today, does anybody have the courage to challenge the ruler of the day?"

".........."

"Baba Nanak has been acknowledged as the incarnation of Kaliyug. When the mother earth started groaning under the weight of sins, she approached the Almighty who said, 'Do you cry because of unbearable weight on you?' The mother Earth said, 'No my Lord, I don't feel the weight of even the mountains. What burdens me most is the ungrateful men.' And those were the days when the sages who were supposed to guide humanity like a light-house had hidden themselves in the caverns of mountains. Then God sent Guru Nanak to redeem Earth from the mire of sins."

"Great, great is the Almighty", some of the listeners said in unison.

"Bhai Gurdas is known as the avtar of Ved Vyas. Bhai Gurdas mentions that moment: Suni pukar daatar prabhu, gur Nanak Jag mahi Pathaya. (The God listened to the supplication of Mother Earth and sent Guru Nanak to this world) Jab Jab hove dharm ghulami, tab dar aai avtar mahani (As and when religion gets enslaved to irreligion, then some great avatar descends on the earth.) Gurbani writes Satijug tain manyo, Chhal bal Bavan bhayo, Trete tain manyo, Ram Raghuvans kahayo, Dwapar Krishan murar kans kritarth kiyo, Uggar Sain kau raaj abhay bhagtah jan (46) diyo, Kaliyug praman Nanak gur Angad, Amar Kahayo (O God! You came on this earth in satyug as Baavan avtar- the trickster god, in treta as Rama of Raghuvansh, in Dwapar as Krishna to free humanity from the tyranny of Kans and restore the kingdom to Uggar Sain to the great relief of his devotees and in Kaliyug as Guru Nanak, Guru Angad and Guru Amar Das. That is why Guru Nanak is known as the avtar of Kaliyug-Aap narain kala dhar jag meh parvareo (God Himself came to the world in disguise). Then you know well, Jis ke sir ooper tu swami, so dukh kaisa paavei (he who enjoys your patronage O Lord, is immune to all suffering). It was then at last that Mother earth had a sigh of relief. Mann chao bhaya prabhu aagam suniya. (As she heard about the advent of God, her joy knew no bounds).

"........."

The Giani's words pacified the hearts of otherwise agitated listeners.

"Baba Nanak himself went to the sinners to redeem them. Unlike the impostors of today, he did not make people fall at his feet. He carried out four odyssies on foot, humbled the pride of people like Vali Kandhari and transformed demons like Kauda. He condemned Babar but embraced the lepers."

As per his habit, Giani Pooran Singh delivered a lengthy speech. A good gathering had converged there.

Giani Pooran Singh's arrival was a great solace to all of them. He had a knack of satisfying them with references from Gurbani or the parables from Guru Gobind Singh's life.

He exhorted all to recite 'Waheguru Waheguru." The recitation of Gurbani had in a way, boosted their morale. It seemed as if they had got a messiah in the form of Giani Pooran Singh.

The allotment officer reached on the third day. He was short-statured and sported a cowl-turban. He had a habit of touching his curled moustache time and again. His legs were as slender as sugarcanes but still they supported his protuberant paunch

very successfully. Some extra flesh of feet looked hanging out of his shoes. Looking at the refugees, he shrank his nose occasionally as if they exuded some stench.

"This man looks very whimsical kind," the Giani said in a whisper to Hazoor Singh.

"Just see how he twists his face."

"I think he will create some new problem," said Thamman

"Yes! And a big one," The amli said

Inder, the chowkidar called aloud and all the camp-dwellers gathered near the allotment officer.

"Listen, listen to me brothers….." brandishing the mulberry twig held in his hand, the chowkidar said.

A silence gripped the whole atmosphere as the people stopped talking to each other.

"Come closer a bit, you can resume these talks later on also.

The campers drew closer like a herd of cows.

"He is our big Sahib. Govt. has appointed him to rehabilitate the families dislodged from Pakistan. You are to get the area of landed property you had in Pakitan. Next week assessment will be complete and on its basis the allotments will be made. Now come one by one please and get your previous name and address as also your property left behind in Pakistan recorded.

As the Chowkidar concluded his directive, the officer picked up the thread.

"Listen, you all ! My name is Har Narayan." Report to me only that much property which was actually there in Pakistan. You Know I can't tolerate lies? And I am very strict with the liars- Understand?"

All bowed their heads.

The procedure commenced. Name, address, father's name, amount of possession and details of loss of life.

By evening almost twenty five percent of the procedural work was complete. The rest was left on the next day and the officer departed with the chowkidar.

Those left behind felt duped and silent.

"Is he Har Narain or what?" The amli broke the silence.

"Says' you know I don't tolerate lies? How can we? Are you our Bhua's[20] son?"

"And says, 'Report only as much property as you had."

"I say, we should be thankful even if we get half of what we had," the Giani said. He did not believe in unequitable distribution.

"I think they won't do anything at all. It will only be an eye wash." Hazoor Singh was very sad at the prevailing situation."

"What kind of freedom is this? They separated man from man and ruined the happily living people."

"And moreover the daughters and sisters of both sides were molested." The Giani spoke again. He was perturbed more spiritually than economically.

"Oye they have forgotten the devastation and just harp on one thing ; our country has become free; Giani ji, these wounds will not heal throughout our life. The native place left behind in Pakistan will keep pricking in the heart like a rusted nail," the amli said.

---

[20] Father's sister.

"Amlia this is what I used to say daily. Now see everything is before your eyes. It is just as a man sitting in a barber's seat asked him about the length of his hair. The barber said that he should wait a little and all the hair will be before his eyes in no time. It's all politics. On one hand Jinnahism and on the other Nehruism. Both the sides have occupied seats of power. And ruin has come to our share only. Daily a statement comes, "Now our country will progress and prosper." They need be given one blow of a club on the temple and brought here to see the plight of

refugees in their prosperous country." The Giani had flared up like this for the first time.

"But who can ask the mighty to do or not to do anything?"

"It's not that Mussalmans have suffered less in any way. Some of them have lost their families. What is worth thinking is whether any of Nehru's or Jinnah's relatives has died. Who died and who were those who are ruined? The innocent common people only."

"Oi who stopped or opposed freedom? But at least this loss, this disaster could be averted," rued the amli.

"They got youths like Bhagat Singh killed just to clear their way to the throne. Those who called them radicals, extremists will pay glowing tribute to them for garnering votes," the Giani prophesied.

The allotment officer's procedure continued for a full week. Everyday, he would narrate something new. The people felt vexed but kept their cool. And what could they do after all? It was a question of their children's future. Uprooted they already were. Then why to annoy the officer-on-the-spot? Reeling under the heavy wheels of destiny, they compromised over such things. These men of enviable self esteem put up with so many things with a heroic fortitude.

People were very much agitated with the allotment officer.

"You see Hazoor Singh, who bothered for such dirty fellows earlier? Amli world say in utter exasperation.

"Amlia when lion collapses due to injuries, then jackal becomes the king. And a squirrel is the leader. The time is like this, what to do?" Hazoor Singh was helpless. Always trying to digest poison like a beaten snake.

"Nobody ever dared stand before us." Thamman Nodded the head is frustration.

"These are descendents of Gangu, my dear ones," the Giani said.

People started pestering the chowkidar. He too was helpless.

"I am also one amongst you my brother," he said and broke away from them with great difficulty.

"Only the officers themselves know their ways," he would say. He also felt sorry for the uprooted ones but he could do nothing. He was in the job against his conscience. A human heart throbbed in his chest also. His soul cried. But to wake both ends meet, he was pulling on with the job. He stifled his conscience. But he could not sleep during the whole night. If at all he had a nap, the sight of famished faces frightened him out of his sleep. So he would make up with a jerk.

Khichdi[21] was served twice only in the camp. Canal water was used for drinking. The campers would see hundreds of dead bodies floating in the canal. But still they had to drink its water out of compulsion.

The camp received more help from the nearby villages than government.

The villagers supplied gur, tea wheat (flour and other essential commodities to the camp. The philanthropic people treated the 'mouth of the hungry as the Guru's coffer.' Therefore, they contributed their mite to the camp. Some benevolent women would bring the chapattis and fed the children and the aged themselves. They would bring them milk and attend the sick wholeheartedly.

---

[21] A dish of rice mixed with lentil

When their hunger was satisfied the people showered a torrent of blessings on them.

"This world rests on the nobility of such people only," Giani Bachan Singh said.

"O yes, otherwise would it not have perished by now?" Thamman dittoed the idea.

After fifteen days, the allotement incharge again came to the camp. This time he was accompanied with another man of his own like.

The people thronged to him with a new hope.

The chowkidar was also present on the occasion.

The people talking to each other stopped at the signal of the officer.

"Well, refugee brothers! I have assessed all your possessions. The record has been sent to the higher authorities. Allotment-letters-will come duly attested from there. And from today onwards, Sardar Tota singh (looking at the man standing with him) will be the allotment officer. He is your Punjabi brother. As and when the allotment-letters come attested from above, you will get your allotted land and house."

"How many days will it take sir?" Thamman asked.

"It all depends on the higher authorities. May be the orders arrive tomorrow or it may take months also." Now instead of the earlier incharge, Tota Singh replied.

All of them became awfully silent to hear this.

"Sircar, the high officers are not to do much but putting signatures on the allotment. Ask them to finish with it." Hazoor Singh's request was interspersed with taunt.

"Had it been in my competency. I would have allotted you the entire Pakistan," Tota Singh also reciprocated ironicathy.

"What to speak of Pakistan Sircar! There we lived like princes. We ate well and used to have a sound sleep. It's only this bloody 'Freedom' which has made us paupers," the amli said and silenced Tota Singh.

When seiged even a tom-cat tears aparts the hunter. Thinking so, the allotment officer took his register and slipped away.

The people were caught in a very strange situation.

Tota singh visited the camp twice in a week and went away after giving them a new promise every time. One day, he came along with a munshi[22]. The pyjama she wore was so loose that it seemed as if it was not the munshi who wore it but the otherway round. Air war traveling fast in and out of his double-barrel like nostrils. And he seemed as restless as a buffalo who is about to deliver any time.

"Munshi Ji," Tota Singh said.

"Yes Sir?" The munshi whimpered like a newt.

"Read out the instructions to them."

"Right Sir."

The munshi got up. He cleared his throat and put on glasses like the blinders of a camel running the Persian wheel . His devilish eyes looked rotating behind the thick glasses.

Rasting his chin on the curved handle of his thick club, the amli was watching his body language very intently.

"Brothers!" saying this he took out a big-sized paper from his pocket. His eyes were focused inalienably on the paper.

"Now listen to the instructions from the above allotment will be made on the basis of numbers. The numbers of each and every family will be sent by hand daily to the camp. So brothers, no refugee should waste our time by approaching us without numbers. The process will start from tomorrow. Wherever a family is allotted land it will have to go there. The whole of India is ours. Whoever

---

[22] Clerk

raises any objection regarding the allotted lands or picks up a dispute, will have to go at the fag end of the line and wait far longer. The landed quota may also exhaust. And then the man will have to repent a lot. So wisdom lies in the acceptance of wherever land is allotted. At last I would request once again to all of you not to come without allotment number. It will be of no use. You will be simply wasting your time and ours."

Thus issuing instructions and threats they left.

"Lo, do what you can to them now."

"Want allotment from them! Hunh…"

"Yaar, why not first teach them a lesson? Everyday, they are putting us off in one way or the other. Let them also face the heat of weather a bit," Said the amli rotating, the curved handle of his club under the chin.

"First see what they are up to. Don't be foolish like this," The Giani admonished them.

"A day after tomorrow is not far."

"Keep silent till then."

"Baba if a day after tomorrow also they show their nakedness, then?" A youngman addressed Giani Ji in a way that lacked due respect for the elders.

"Then beta you are free to fire whatever machinegun you have," said Giani ji in a very calm and composed manner. It made the impudent youngman speechless at once.

"Quarreling won't do any good at all."

The boy remained silent.

And it was right also. Who could resist the state? Any resistance would have recoiled on them only. The allotment officer and munshi were the representatives of government. In exasperation, they would have no scruples in rejecting a case or at least remark 'Rejected by the refugee.' Who could stop them. They were the authorities at that time. What can one do if camel does not sit with love words Ichh Ichh' from the owner. Nobody can make it sit with force. So at times, silence is golden. This human tongue needs great care in its usage. Otherwise it is ready to throw you out of the village once used in an indiscreet manner. So any kind of untoward reaction would be harming yourself. And the harassment thereupon as an extra 'bonus.' Patience and self control was the only way out in that situation.

"Moreover, if you create any nuisance it will only give them an excuse to be hard on us." The amli said very wisely.

"Kabira sangat kariye saadh ki, gussa mann na handhai. Dehi rog na laggai, palle sabh kichh pai," (The great poet Kabir says that: O man, sit in the company of the rightleous. Don't feel angered at heart. This self-restraint will keep your body free of all ailments and help you achieve all that you cherish. The Giani said, "So my dear keep your fire under contol."

The Giani was fully alive to the agony of the dislodged people. But losing cool at such times too could be suicidal. How could the uprooted lot face the might of the state?

"Baba ji, I am really sorry. But hunger knows no etiquette, what to do? Where shall we kill ourselves? Enjoying like princes in our own homes, we are sitting here like the gypsies," The youngman said with a sense of repentance and frustration at the sametime.

"The very people from whose doorsteps nobody ever turned hungry, are now worried about their own daily bread," spoke another victim of 'freedom'.

"My dear ones, I am well aware of your woes. I am in no way, a less sufferer than you. But we should express our anger only where it works," the Giani sprinkled cold water on the inflamed passions. The farmers, who left in their full-grown crop, a share for the birds, the passers by and the poor, were looking towards the government with a begging bowl. Only the villagers had a real feel of their suffering.

They were contented with a bowl of Khichdi and a glass of water as their daily diet these days.

The third day, as informed by the munshi, also came and only three families got their numbers.

It sent a wave of frustration among the camp-dwellers.

The munshi came with his usual professional arrogance and returned after making allotments to three families.

The incharge did not come at all.

"It this remains the pace of allotment, it will take a full year." The amli calculated the time of allotment in his mind.

"We shall starve to death by that time." some other said.

"Don't be so hasty. Wait for a day or two. Then we shall meet the incharge." The Giani advised.

All agreed to him

The number of allotments kept increasing day by day. But the number did not exceed ten.

One month passed like his

The helpless sufferers started pressing upon the incharge. Their sense of tolerance was exhausted now. The sick members of their families were an additional liability on them.

Santi's condition was as it earlier was.

There was no improvement in Melo's hysterical outbursts.

The suffering of people was unfathomable indeed!

Amli, Hazoor Singh and Thamman approached the allotment-officer.

"Sircar, tell us something about our allotment also," said amli with utmost humility.

"You have got on my nerves, yaar."

"Sardar ji it's five days and a month now. We come daily and go back disappointed."

"You mean, you oblige me by coming here? Helping you under your pressure will not do?" The incharge came in his usual bureaucratic form.

"Sircar, we are the dispossessed ones."

"So ? Shall I fix a monthly pension for you?"

"Sircar, it's for the government to do everything. You are to put your signatures only."

"Now you are teaching me the law?"

"What type of law can we teach you sircar! Even my forefathers didn't know a bit of it. They also perished in gross neglect. Sircar, we are the ones to salute you and beg of you only."

"Okay, come after your number comes."

"Sircar, please be merciful. Who knows when the number is going to come."

"I say, come after you get your number. Get lost now… Munshi….."

"Yes Sir."

"Let nobody come here without number. If this bloody cougher comes here without number, give him a blow on his temple."

"Yes sir."

"Now listen to me with open ears…"

The officer looked at the amli with his mouth ajar like a wolf.

"If again you come here without number, you will be given such a thrashing that you will ask for life."

"…….." The amli was looking stunned at the officer.

"We'll write to the government that nobody by the name of Baghtu amli lives in the camp. Then you will be free to do what you like. Understand?"

"……." Earth seemed slipping from under his feet. Then all of a sudden, shouting and howling like a frightened ghost he ran towards the fields.

All of them came back frustrated.

"Say what was bad about living in Pakistan? At least we had a respectful living, doing our own work and eating peacefully," said Thamman to Hazoor Singh.

"What to say just doing and having a respectful living, it was a life full of great enjoyment." Hazoor Singh, too, was very fed up with the slack pace of allotment. His bones could be heard crackling in his feeble frame covered with rags.

"What bloody freedom is this? It has made us sit with begging bowls like street beggars."

"Let the Yama1 take you to hell, you politician swines… May you not wake up alive in the morning." The amli was wailing, sitting near the bullock-cart.

"For their own political power you made the people of both sides kill each…. And made thousands homeless."

His lamentation pierced everybody's heart. His wounds had started suppurating. That is why he was hurling curses on the rulers.

"O God! This 'freedom' has made us beggars….." Amli's grief touched everybody. Beside outward ruin, there was a storm in his very being as well.

"They themselves sit under the ceiling fans to make decision," Santu said," all smiles they say on the radio, "Azadi ki mubarak ho' (Happy independence)."

"They should be dragged from Delhi and brought here to see their misdoings." Jaagar felt agitated and slapped himself in this very mood.

So many people had gathered there to hear this dialogue.

"And see this incharge and his munshi. Don't know what they think of themselves. For a full month they have been befooling us." Santu said beating his chest.

"Shouldn't we knock down the munshi tonight?" Amli gripped his bludgeon hard as he said.

"Don't be foolish. We shall get deprived of whatever allotment has to be made."

"Doesn't matter. Already we are not enjoying a very comfortable life." The amli started making sit-ups in fury. His nerves had stiffened.

"You foolish Jatts…!" the Giani said, " impotent fury does no good at all. We have already suffered a lot. Let us see that suffering doesn't become our destiny here at least."

"……."

"It's the doing of leaders for which we have to suffer now."

"What's the solution then?"

"Friends! The elders used to say in the past that a day would come when a lamp will be seen shimmering at not less than twelve kohs[23]. Now see this is what is happening before our eyes."

"The words of elders are never without meaning."

"Oi Santu!"

"Oi where has Santu died?"

Pilla was seen coming from the other side, mumbling in bewilderment.

"Oi what has gone wrong, you! man with dirty eyes?"

"Santi has fainted again."

"She has become another trouble for me….. She just adds to my misery," Said Santu, gnashing his teeth like an ill-tempered camel.

---

[23] A unit of distance equal to approximately 2.4 kms.

"Oi, she doesn't do this knowingly. Nobody has any control over the disease," the Giani said.

"Her young and only son has been killed Giani Ji. The root of the family tree is cut-off. Happily living, we all have been pushed out of our places. Nobody is to blame brother. Let's go and take care of her…"

"Giani Ji, suffering is right on its side. But now shall we hang ourselves or bear with the situation?"

"Don't lose heart. Come let's go and see her."

All of them rushed towards the camp.

This is the fortitude of Punjabis that they steel their hearts even in the midst of trials and tribulations.

They never lose courage.

Santu went and opened her jaw-lock with the help of a spoon. When some drops of water were poured into her mouth, she opened her eyes. Lying on the wet grass she was looking at all with the eyes of a stranger, as if in dementia. Her lackluster eyes had become sunken like jackal pits.

"Hasn't Pala come so far?" she asked in a very feeble voice.

"………" All looked at her with interrogative eyes- as if Santi had frightened them.

They stood bewildered.

The question had hit them like a brick. Nobody had any answer to it. They seemed to have fallen prostrate in a dark abyss.

"Those who leave, never come back Santi. Don't grieve so much. Remember the name of God!" Har Kaur tried to control the situation. But she failed as words fail to become a solace for the aggrieved in such a situation.

"What God Bebe ji? I don't find myself comfortable with Him. Pala has sat heavy on my chest. Ha!" said Santi and started wailing.

"Ve, the butchers hacked you my handsome child……"

"………"

"I kept nourishing you with milk and butter O child….."

"………."

"Ve, I brought you up only for the wolves, my son……Ha!"

"……….." The eyes of all were filled with tears. The lamentations of Santi were piercing everybody's heart.

The women of the whole camp started weeping for their respective dead.

There prevailed an atmosphere of hue and cry.

It looked more like a cremation-ground than a camp. Everybody had his or her own loss to mourn. The air reverberated with heart-rending lamentation.

"Have patience now Santi. Be courageous. The Guru will do good. Take water and be at peace…!" Har Kaur tried to make her drink water by supporting Santi's head with her arm but due to sobs most of the water came out of her mouth corners

The well-built, six-feet high youths were standing with their eyes full of tears. Someone was shedding tears silently and wiping them with an ashen shoulder-cloth.

"Santu" A perplexed Har Kaur said.

"Yes Tai[24]….?"

"Call the doctor. She has again got unconscious." Santu hurriedly went to the camp doctor. Gurmukh opened the jaw-lock of Santi.

Har Kaur again made her drink water. Santi was in bad condition.

All were worried.

---

[24] Fem. Of Taya i.e. father's elder brother

"Giani Ji, I am overstepping my shoes" said amli in a subdued tone.

"Don't conceal anything you want to say."

"I think Santi will breathe her last today." Amli said and looked all around.

"Marn likhai mandal meh aai." Gurbani says that man comes into this world by first having got his death destined."

"You are hundred percent right Giani ji. But one doesn't want to die in desolation either. You should die where there are some people to weep for you."

"That is also right, but when one dies how does it matter whether one dies on a royal bed or in desolation?"

Amli became silent

Doctor arrived.

He felt the pulse

He gave pudis[25] of medicine

The doctor directed to administer one pudi in the morning and one in the evening.

"Make her lie in the open outside. It is very humid inside. Half of the ailment is due to this only. Bring him out of the tent and keep giving her water after short intervals." The doctor gave instructions and went away.

Thus the unconscious Santi was brought into open. Now she had gained some consciousness and had taken a pudi also.

The night fell.

Today, Daal-Chawal (pulse and rice) were cooked in the camp. All the campers took their food and returned to their respective tents. The rain that fell a day earlier, had made slush all around. The mosquitoes were another problem to deal with.

---

[25] The paper packings of medicine.

The cattle would do with whatever little fodder was given to them. At times they would lock horns also. They no longer had energy to fight with each other.

The cattle who were used to eating five kilograms of oil-cakes each also seemed to be cursing the independence.

It being very hot, all men and women started trying to sleep on their carts. The children were crying due to the sultriness of heat in the atmosphere.

The morning came with a good news. Most of the campers had received number. Bachint Kaur, Thamman, Jaagar, Hazoor Singh. Giani ji, Santu, amli, Gurmukh and others marched towards the office of allotment incharge.

Amli did not want to face the officer. But what could he do? He had to meet him by compulsion.

As the sun rose, they reached the office of the allotment officer.

After waiting for about three hours, a new officer appeared today. He was also tight-lipped like others with well-oiled hair and henna-dyed beard. Since he was not an adept hand at dying, his stubble beard looked like the It sitt weed of Bikrami month Ashadh. The munshi had on his shoulders a big heavy register.

"Ram[26]-Ram babu ji[27]...."

All spoke in unison.

"........" Rather than responding, the incharge pursed his lips still more tightly and the munshi laid the register on the table almost as gently as one spreads a bed-sheet.

The incharge kept shuffling the pages of the register for some time. All of them were looking at the officer with folded hands like culprits.

The officer handed over the allotment letters to all of them.

When the munshi read them aloud, they were worried. Bachint Kaur, Gurmukh, Giani ji amli and Santu were allotted land near Amritsar while Hazoor Singh and Thamman got it towards

---

[26] A religious greeting.

[27] An Indian word used both in the meaning of clerk and officer.

Jalandhar somewhere. Jaagar got land and house in a village near Ferozepur.

The men belonging to the same village were divided by the government's orders.

"Babu ji, what shall I do in Ferozepur district alone? Better allot me land alonwith one of my native villagers," Jaagar resented. He could hardly see his village folks departing. He had spent a lot of time and shared joys and sorrows with them. He was standing with tearful eyes before the officer.

"These are government's orders, not mine." The officer said and left the office. The munshi also followed him with the excitement of buffalo eager to be expectant.

Jaagar felt like weeping aloud.

They were looking at each other with helplessness writ large on their faces. Parting with each other looked very difficult to them.

"We must accept what we are given as a gift from God. So move in the name of Waheguru. If God wants we shall meet again. After all we are all in Punjab only. The living beings keep meeting. This is the law of nature. So bow to will of God and move….!" The Giani's words boosted their morale to a certain extent.

Frustrated , they moved towards their carts.

The luggage was loaded on them.

They enquired about the route to their respective allotted villages from the chowkidar, had an assessment of distance and the nature of roads leading to their destination etc.

As the bullock-carts moved, Jaagar could not contain himself and he burst in to sobs and tears.

"Now when are we going to meet, brother…!"

The pangs of separation pulsated in the hearts of all and tears welled up in their already moistened eyes.

"Don't lose heart Jaagra. These are only the ways of God and this is how He will it." The Giani patted his back like pacifying a child.

"Giani Ji, for what sin has God given us this shock of separation. I have never killed even an ant."

Jaagar was weeping inconsolably.

He was not able to contain himself.

All stood sad and dejected.

"Jaagra, don't get late now and don't feel so bad about it. We shall definitely keep meeting. I tell you the scheme.

"We shall converge at Darbar Sahib Amritsar every year on the occasions of Diwali and Baisakhi. Thus we shall be able to have a darshan of Harimandir Sahib and lay bare our hearts to each other. So first try to settle. God will take care, don't worry."

"........." Everybody felt delighted at this proposal.

"Let's move the in the name of Waheguru."

"Well, Santi, we'll meet in Amritsar on Diwali," said Jagar with a bit of elevated spirits.

Santi, lying almost in an unconscious state waved her hand in negative but could say nothing otherwise.

The lackluster eyes of Santi were filled abrim with tears. Her body had become quite frail. Jaagar touched Har Kaur's feet.

A despondent Har Kaur bestowed on him a shower of blessings. The women met by clasping to each other and lightened their hearts by shedding tears.

Anyway, they remembered Waheguru and set out on their unknown journey.

Beaten hard by the adversity of circumstances, They and others reached their destinations.

It was a small village.

The Muslims had migrated from here to Pakistan in large numbers. They too, had suffered a great loss of life……. The deserted houses seemed to tell the woeful tale of their suffering as well. A few Mosques here and there too wore a desolated look A horrible sight indeed.

They came and placed their luggage in different houses.

These stranger houses looked scary to them. ……….. Empty kitchens were frightful. It took them a full week for adjusting the luggage. Gradually, they started adapting themselves to the new conditions.

The extinguished hearths had fire once again. The villages were always ready to help these refugees. Giani Pooran Singh was entrusted service in the village Gurdwara. He would discharge his duties with great devotion and perform a regaling Kirtan1.

After about a couple of weeks, Santi passed away. She had a bad dream in sleep. Frightened she let out a heart-rending shriek calling out," Ve Pala!" and breathed her last. People guessed that she had a heart failure.

Her mortal remains were consigned to the flames.

"Giani Ji!" said Santu to the Giani who had come to condole Santi's death. Further he could not say anything due to choked throat and started weeping.

"Ghalle aay Nanaka, sadde uth jaaye." (you come to this world at the orders of God and then leave here at His call only) Steel your heart. She had only this much age in store." The Giani tried to console the bereaved Santu by quoting from Guru Granth Sahib, the holy scripture.

"That's all right Giani Ji but…….."

"Yes say openly. Why are you hesitating?"

"I say, the deceased has left as per His will nobody can resist that. Why not organize a path (recitation of holy Gurbani) so that her soul should doesn't keep wandering. She never saw any days of joy throught out her life, let her soul rest now at least," saying so, Santu started weeping again.

"Yes, we can do that."

"But Giani ji I have no money for that. What to do? But I feel like having it."

"We'll do this…."

Santu raised his head in curiosity.

"Vadda data til na tmai (God is pleased with devotion not lucre. We'll do a Sehaj Paath[28] in the Gurdwara. At Sangrand we'll organize Bhog ceremony and pray for the departed soul. Why do you worry? Santi was common to served to the village. The food material brought by the Sangat will be Sangat itself."

Santu felt his heart unburdened now.

Although he used to keep quarreling with Santi everyday and at times raised his hand at her as well. But her absence had made him for lorn in the world.

The consecutive deaths of his only young son Pala and then Santi, had broken him altogether.

Giani Pooran Singh held the Sehaj Path in the Gurdwara and concluded it on Sangrand. He himself prayed for the peace of Santi's departed soul.

After the Bhog, the mentally deranged girl Melo's mother Bachint Kaur told the Giani something which swept him off his feet. This unexpected development had hit his brain like a spanner. Melo was pregnant. Bachint Kaur was out of her wits to know this. She failed to think what to do, what would be the outcome of this. She had seen the image of a messiah in the Giani and come to him.

---

[28] As compared to Akhand Path which is a 48 hours incessant recital of the whole Guru Granth Sahib, the Sehaj Path is more flexible. The Sehaj Path takes normally a week or so with the recital of 2-3 hours daily as per convenience.

"Bachint Kaur, why didn't you tell this to me earlier? Now you have come at the eleventh hour.

"Giani Ji, I myself have come to know yesternight only when she started vomiting." She bemoaned.

The Giani was caught in a fix.

He racked his brain a lot but no solution come to his mind on the spur of the moment.

"Giani Ji, find out some or the other solution. She, the poorthing is already stained. Nobody is going to accept her. May heavens fall on the bastard muslas, Giani ji, people will call her child also a progeny of mussalmans. O my God! Where should I hide myself? … Which well should I jump into? You take me away also O God. Bachint Kaur beat her thighs with her both hands and sat down on the ground.

"Bachint Kaur, nobody can stop the inevitable. You do only one thing……. Just go home and let me think something. Have faith in Baba Nanak. He will himself show some way." the Giani consoled Bachint Kaur.

"Baba Nanak ! Please show me some way. Daya Karo kuchh mehar upavo-dubde patthar tare. Have mercy me. You have the power to make the stones float on water. Thus praying, the Giani come to Har Kaur.

"How are you Tai?"

"How can the ones like us be? You know better my son, Pooran Singh."

"That is very clear Tai."

"What brings you here beta?"

"What to say, Tai? When the destiny becomes your enemy, even a rope turns in to a serpant for you. Now a new trouble has come our way, Tai."

"What is that beta?" Har Kaur became serious.

"You know Melo, Bachint Kaur's daughter?"

"Yes, of course."

"The mussalmans roughed her up and she is expecting now."

"Waheguru! Waheguru!"

"Demented she already was and now………."

"Waheguru ! Waheguru!

"And now this new calamity."

"O my true Master!"

"Melo't mother, as they say, is lost from all sides."

"Had her father been alive, he would have made much arrangement. Now what should the lone woman do?"

"She's not to blame beta." Har Kaur nodded her head in great disgust.

"What worries me most Tai is the future of the girl. What will become of her? Stained she already was and now…. Where shall she wash this sin off her?"

"She is not even in a position to bring up her child. The mother too is not normal and keeps weeping all the time."

"What can she do beta?"

For many days the Giani kept thinking about Melo and her mother Bachint Kaur. But while doing so his own heart flickered like the flame of an earthen lamp. The swerved mind was not catching any momentum.

Ultimately he again started rubbing his forehead before the Guru Granth Sahib and prayed to the Master to show him the path. He would even taunt the Almighty.

One day, Harkaur called him through a messenger. The Giani appeared before her at once.

"Santu has lost his wife and son at such an early age. He is just forty years of age," Har Kaur said.

"............" The Giani was silent. He was engrossed deep in his thoughts.

"Beta, his mother didn't keep very good health. So she married him off at a tender age and he came under the yoke of household liabilities. And then you know......."

"But Tai, Santu is double the age of Melo."

"So what beta? No young boy is going to accept her. She will be accepted only by some needy person. You can try in the whole area near around. If anybody even listens to this proposal properly, you change my name. The people have only lip-sympathy for others, beta."

"Tai ! Won't the society say so many nasty things about this mismatching?"

"This is the way of the world beta. The people must say something or the other. Who has ever pleased society? It laughs with the laughing but won't shed a tear for the miserable. You see, for how many days Bachint Kaur has been crying. Has anybody come to ask her well being? So if you listen to me, get the girl married to Santu. After Santi's death he too has become very lonely. The grief of Pala's death has eaten into his entrails already. He is very much grief-stricken at heart but doesn't express. Now after Santi's death, he has become quite speechless."

"But Tai, they are living in the same village. How it will work? The people will say so many things."

"Beta, they have settled in the same village only after they were displaced from their homes. Otherwise, there is a distance of about twenty kohs between their native villages. If you are to give the girl a safe future, you will have to bear the foolish jabber of people for a few days. Thereafter, everything will be normal. There is a well-known story normally told by the elderly women of the village.

A newly arrived daughter-in-law of a chamar[29] family used to mind the foul smell pervading the whole atmosphere. Cleaning or

---

[29] A lowcaste engaged in peeling off the dead animals and tanning of leather, cobbler.

dusting the house, she would shrink her nose in disgust. In due course of time she got used to the smell. But she told the people with pride, "I have cleaned the house so well that no doubt, it has taken a full month but I have freed the house of all the stench." Similarly, the jabber of people will stop itself within a few days. And you know, Inder of our previous village Malaudan had married a weaver woman of the some village. The people wagged their tongues for some days. And now it's the same Inder and same village. He died as a man having sons and grandsons."

Harkaur's argument had a substance and so convinced the Giani.

"Moreover, beta she is a young jatt lass. What to fear from man!"

The Giani succumbed to Harkaur's wisdom.

"Tai, you do one thing."

"Say, beta."

"Women can talk such things to women more easily. You just touch this proposal with Bachint Kaur. Rest I will take care."

"Don't worry, I will talk to her. It's a question of village daughter's after all. It's an act of great virtue."

The Giani walked towards the Gurdwara.

Harkaur went to Bachint Kaur.

"How are you Bachint Kaur?"

Sitting on the peehri[30] Har Kaur asked.

"How can someone like me, be after all? It's only a little short of death, nothing else." Bachint Kaur was very dejected. In extreme desperation, she started weeping.

"Today, I had talked to Pooran Singh…….. come on, sit near me."

She spoke in a tone of whisper.

---

[30] A low stringed stool

Bachint Kaur drew closer to her.

"How's Melo?"

"Now she is a little better. Now she doesn't act much like mad as before…. Not does she explode like earlier now." Hope she will get well But Bebe ji, the stain that she has. you know…" said Bachint Kaur with a hand on her chest as if trying to save her heart from sinking.

"Bachint Kaur, calamities are always uninvited and unavoidable. One has to taste the bitter cup of life many a time. Your Baba was full ten years older than I and I was quite young. You know sister, the girl has to live with the man the parents choose for her. Why tell a lie, your Baba took great care of me. He never turned down my word."

"………" Bachint Kaur listened to her silently.

"Once Bachint, I insisted for going to see the Baloch fair. The someday it was our turn to get canal water for the wheat crop. Moreover, some marriage was to be attended. But he didn't say 'no' to me. Harnessing the camel, he accompanied me. As regards wheat field, he sent the farm laborers to get it watered and the marriage was attended by his elder brother. We returned from the fair on the third day. And he bought me a beautiful nala[31] studded with mirrors.

"…………"

"You know why I have come to you."

"Yes Bebe?"

"I had talked to Pooran Singh about our Melo. Santi, you know has died just recently. Santu only looks aged, otherwise he is only forty. He has played in my lap. Furthermore, he is needy and all alone. Actually. I am talking of him in respect of our Melo.

Bachint Kaur got lost in thoughts : "Was my melo destined for Santu only? Oh, such a bad luck! But there is no way out either. Santu is still better choice than falling into a river. We have no

---

[31] A cord used for fastening the trousers, underwear etc.

support in the world. At least, Santu will become one. A drowning man even catches at a straw. To live life one needs some or the other support. No wall can keep erect without a foundation. How shall I keep the demented Melo with her illegitimate child? The youngster sons have been killed. The husband too, has deserted me. So I must savour this bitter pill." She felt herself being swayed by a current of thoughts.

"What are you thinking of?" As Har Kaur shook her out of her thinking self, she came back to the world of realism.

"Look, if you are thinking of his mature age, then it's up to you. But Santu is not a bad man. He can sacrifice his blood for you. I have known him ever since he was a child. He will love the girl from the core of his heart, this much I can assure."

"Bebe ji, I will do as you and Giani ji say," Bachint Kaur said halfheartedly.

"Dyal's son Bakhtaura of our village got widower after fifteen years of his marriage. His in-laws were so gentle that they married their youngest daughter to him. And he had been fondling her as a child. But the same girl bore three very beautiful and healthy sons from Bakhtaura. God will take care Bachint Kaur. And Santu listens to me what I ask him to do. He is very nice at heart. You will know when you deal with him. If at all you have anything against him in future, come to me. I am responsible."

Bachint Kaur agreed.

"If you agree to me Bebe ji, I am ready to make her sit for Anand Karaj[32] right tomorrow but……" Bachint Kaur stopped saying something.

"You say what you have to. I am listening. Only man helps man, say without any hesitation."

"Bebe ji what I fear most is that he may taunt my daughter over illegitimate child, calling it muslas' off spring."

---

[32] Sikh ceremony of wedding.

"I' will make him bald by the blows of shoes on his head if he says anything of this kind. You just know one thing. Ever since Santi died, he is out to seek the support of even the walls. You will be a great support to her and when Melo goes to his house, he will be able to contain himself."

".........."

"The new bride is more intoxicating than even datura for man. You will see how he hovers around Melo. Catch hold of me if he doesn't. Moreover, our Melo is very beautiful."

"Anyway Bebe ji, I am with you and Giani ji. I will accept what you say. But you will have to own the entire responsibility."

"Bachint Kaur, don't worry on this count. I will talk to Santu," getting up she said.

"Bebe ji, Santu doesn't know so far?" Bachint Kaur was astonished.

"No, not yet. It is only I and Pooran Singh who had thought it all. It's a question of girl's life after all. You leave all worrying. It's for me to persuade Santu. He won't say 'no' The poorthing is all alone. If you offer water to a thirsty man, why shall he refuse?"

Har Kaur left. As Bachint Kaur looked carefully at Melo, she felt greatly agonized at heart.

"You should have got good fortune also along with a pretty face." She said caressing Melo's forehead in an impassioned manner.

Melo started staring intently at her mother. Now she had controlled herself absolutely. There were no outbursts of dementia. She now ate food and drank milk or tea. She would also wash her clothes and at the bidding of her mother, she visited the Gurdwara also.

After Santi's death Santu had lost all zest for life. His feelings had become dormant. He did not feel like going to the allotted land. The house without Santi had become like a body without soul for him-devoid of life altogether.

The amli would pay a visit to her off and on. It made him feel comfortable when they emptied their hearts to each other. At times, amli would bring a bottle of country liquor. Drinking till midnight they raked their common past and wept by clinging to each other's heart. The garbage of unwholesome memories was washed with their tears.

Santu had hardly finished with serving the gutava[33] to the bullocks when Tai Har Kaur came.

"What are you doing beta Santu?"

"Just finished with feeding gutava to the bullocks Tai." "Well done. Both the farmer and the bullock depend on each other for their subsistence. This relation is also pre-ordained. beta," sitting on the cot she said

"Shall I prepare tea for you Tai?"

"Yes, make it and you also keep company with me. Santu placed tea-pan on the hearth.

Meanwhile, Har kaur took a round of the whole house Santu brought tea in glasses.

"Tea, we shall take afterwards. First listen to me." Har Kaur touched the issue.

"Yes Tai?"

"You know Melo, Bachint Kaur's daughter?"

---

[33] Chaff, straw of fodder mashed with solution of oil-cake, ground grain etc. and water.

"Yes Tai."

"What do you think about her?"

"What kind of thinking Tai?"

"You are quite naïve just child-like. Your fool! What do you think about marriage with her."

"Marriage is all right Tai, but who is marrying her?" Santu had not been able so far to read between the lines.

"You are really a fool! You will marry Melo, who else." Har Kaur told him in an explicit manner.

"Her marriage with me Tai?" He said with his mouth agape. His eyes had dilated with wonderment and the hair on his head stood erect like the quills of porcupine.

"Yes, with you."

"Tai?" He could not speak further as a vibration had travelled all over his body. He was bewildered for the moment. "Tai why do you ruin the already ruined ? You know my circumstances." His palms were wet with perspiration. He was looking at Har Kaur very helplessly.

In the meanwhile, the Tai was assessing the whole situation very meticulously.

"Tai just see my age and her age!" His heart was pounding fast in his chest.

"Ve, what has gone wrong with your age. You are not much bigger than a child. You have been playing in my lap. It's not a thing of very remote past when you used to urinate on me," The Tai teased him..

"......" Santu could not think anything. He was caught unawares. He blushed with shyness before the elderly aunt.

"You know what trauma the girl has undergone at the hands of muslas."

"That I know Tai."

"Then listen carefully….." She started saying after a pause. "The girl is expectant now. So it will be of benefit to both of you. It will provide the child with paternal love and your own house will start throbbing with life. You will eat the food prepared by her while now you yourself burn your hands preparing chapattis. You have no big age as yet. The Zaildar of our village had married at the age of sixty- the second marriage and that too inspite of his wife being very much alive."

"Tai what will the people say?"

"Hell with the people! Who comes now to bake your chapattis?"

"………"

"Has anybody ever come to enquire about your well-being ever since Santi has died?"

"Tai, I am already overaged" Santu vented his only apprehension with great difficulty."

"Man and horse, they say, never grow old if they keep eating well. By the time Melo comes, you will become as nimble as a horse. She will also get well. And alone you will collapse in not a very long time. So have courage. The men have always been re-building their homes in such cases."

"Tai, will it look good to get married at this age?"

"Ve, it will not be a marriage of much fanfare. You will sit for Anand Karaj, have four rounds of ceremonial circum-ambulations and go home with your bride to live at peace."

"What is the view of Melo's mother?"

"Everybody agrees. Only you are saying this and that." Har Kaur said and starting cooling her tea.

"You get ready-I am going to Pooran Singh." Having finished tea Har Kaur left hastily.

Santu was all agog with joy but was caught in a dilemma.

In the evening he served fodder to the cattle and walked towards the amli.

"I was thinking of coming to you", said amli and in a hilarious mood fished out a bottle of liquor. He brought water from the well and took two brass glasses.

"To what extent is the hush-hush talk about you true?" The amli asked while uncorking the bottle.

"What hush-hush talk?"

"About your marriage, what else? Why do you talk in a round-about way? Tell me in plain words without any circumvention." Saying this the amli poured the country brew into the glasses.

"Earlier Tai left no stone unturned in putting me to shame now you do your heart's will. Only the poor are subjected to humiliation", Santu said and picked the glass.

"Be a man and don't step back now. You had not disappointed as stout a woman as Santi. She is just a child in compartison."

Both of them emptied their glasses and by way of snacks they started eating the freshly uprooted green onions like an ox. The country drink had given them a kick. The sound of their chewing the onions was clearly audible in the stillness of atmosphere.

"This is what I am also afraid about lest under the sway of liquor some day she should become my victim." Santu was really feeling a good kick of the first peg.

"Now don't boast like a wrestler either. Your bones are crackling now. If woman decides once, she refuses to be tamed in the bed. So take care so that you have not to be removed lying dead from above her." The amli divested Santu of all his intoxication with a single stroke.

"Amlia, you miss no chance of letting one down. You have marred all the enjoyment of the first peg. Come pour antoher peg now."

"As much as you like. After all we are not to take it anywhere else. One more bottle is still lying. We shall drink to our full satisfaction today. But one thing you must bear in mind", said amli while filling the glass again.

"………" Santu got alert to hear him.

"Better come home after a single ploughing in the field rather than spending the whole day there but don't ever let your wife feel disappointed. If you failed to satisfy her, she will try to seek sexual gratification somewhere else and then keep you under her thumb. So take care!" They emptied their glasses and started chewing the onions again.

"Don't mind chhote bhai[34] I am saying all this only in my elderly capacity." Due to the influence of liquor, the amli was lisping in his speech. His eyes had turned red."

"No no, I don't mind your saying at all. But I have only one apprehension in my mind."

"Yes ? you just speak out. I won't disappoint you." The amli said. He was looking at Santu like an owl.

"………" Santu was silent.

"Oi, chhote bhai, we can flush out the whole Pakistan with a single jet of urine and if we blow, we can blow up Lahore. You simply say what you have to without hesitation, I will show you the way. What makes you frustrated for nothing? The brothers have always been laying down their lives for brothers. You only order me. I will auction my life for you." The influence of liquor had made amli very strong at heart.

"What I fear, amlia, is this that there may arise a situation that I go near her and she raises a hue and cry to gather the neighbors. She is a bit mentally disturbed."

Amli released a guffaw of laughter at this.

"Oh ho! Is this what you are worried about ? You are making a mountain out of a mole hill. You have not changed a bit."

---

[34] Younger brother

Amli drew closer to Santu.

"Listen to me."

"…………"

"You should pamper her for three four days. Help her in cooking food. Don't try to be violent. The woman has to be won over slowly. There is a lot of difference between consent and coercion. I can under stand her also. The muslas have done great excesses on her. For milking a buffalo, one way is to control her with a stick and the other is by putting green fodder before it. Don't you see the difference? You see how a squeaking wheel gets smooth going once it is greased. So you will see when she starts getting grease, all her madness will go away. She will hesitate for a day of two but then will come to her senses. You are a farmer yourself. You know when a buffalo is to be given hope, she goes to the extent of pulling out her peg. And she becomes very docile as she gets expectant. So the sex becomes an obsession for man. Once it finds an outlet, man is at peace. Why do the young girls have epileptic fits? Due to the same reason. Similarly, when the lioness gets restless, she starts lying in the way and when the she-elephant is possessed with sex, she pulls out the tree. The ancient sadhus and sages would come sitting under the trees where they sat for meditation. So the nature has not made this easing way for nothing. The animals may know or may not know anything else but they definitely know this act."

Santu laughed at this.

"There is nothing to laugh in it chhote bhai. Not even this world can continue for long without it. But those who treat it only as a urine pipe are enemies to nature even though they are saints or sages."

"Santu laughed still more aloud."

"You are laughing like kids. Just think-the cows daily move in the herd but the bull remains averse to them. But when a cow has its days to be expectant, it follows her. This is the law of nature or else there is no meter fitted in the bull to tell him what the cow wants.

Santu could hardly help laughing and spilling out his peg from his mouth.

"One realizes the essence of elders wisdom and taste of the anwla[35] only later on. You can laugh at me if you like but this is the truth."

"What will be the fate of the child to come?" A laughing Santu became serious now.

"Bring it up as a gift of God. Never let any frown appear on your forehead. Every child brings along its destiny. It's a divine being after all. Who knows what is in store for it. So never spurn his gift. Baba Gurditta used to narrate a story that Maharaja Ranjit Singh's mother had been buried by her parents at the time of birth. They did'nt need a daughter. A saint came and told the parents that she will bear such a gallant son who will be known far and wide for his valiance. And you know how he kept the moghuls always on their heels. He used to challenge them by reaching their doorstep. Unfortunately he lost his position due to the betrayal of Dogras. But so long as he lived he didn't allow anybody to raise an evil eye towards Punjab. Strange are the ways of Nature. That is why the wise say that it's up to you. If you make woman work in a cattle-shed, she is a servant but if you make her sit on the throne, she is queen. The scriptures say that nobody has been able to demystify nature. Great are the ways of God. Don't worry, you pick up the glass and have the peg."

Santu felt light at heart. He was sitting carefreely before the amli. Amli's reasoning had infused a new life in him.

Talking to each other they finished two bottles. Santu spent that night at amli's house. Due to the influence of liquor or perhaps lightness of mind, he had a very sound and uninterrupted sleep today. His formidable snores had startled the cow several times but thanks to the rope tangle round her neck, she could not uproot the teher-post. Amli too had been creating weird sounds escaping his lips frequently with the gush of air like a donkey.

---

[35] A medicinal fruit which tastes sour at first but its taste turns sweet in the mouth later on.

The marriage between Santu and Melo was confirmed. The efforts of the Giani and HarKaur had borne fruit. They wanted to see them settled comfortably. God dwelt in human hearts.

Anand karaj was fixed on the day of Sangrand.

On the fixed day, Giani Pooran Singh told the village folks briefly about Melo's background and her tragic deflowering in an implicit manner. He did not want to touch yet unhealed wounds by going in to unnecessary details. He had also not deemed it proper to keep the village people in darkness.

During his brief address he requested the villagers for being compassionate towards Melo and Santu. He had asked them to treat them with love rather than adding to their misery by taunts. All the villagers were very much impressed with the Giani's appeal and everybody had applauded him for his humane attitude.

Anand Karaj ceremony was accomplished. The Giani quoted from Gurbani 'Ek jot doi moorti' (From now onwards the bride and the bridegroom are the same light only manifested in two lamps.) and blessed the couple. The whole village gave Shagun[36] to the newly weds.

Degh[37] was served to the congregation.

"Bebe ji, it doesn't behove me to go to my daughter's house. So you go with her," Bachint Kaur said to Har Kaur. At heart she was feeling very heavy.

"Don't lose heart Bachint Kaur. I will live with Melo for a full week. I say, this is my responsibility." Har Kaur solaced her.

"Bebe ji after all she is my flesh and blood. What if she is a victim of her destiny today." Bachint Kaur's heart was bleeding.

With an aggrieved heart Bachint Kaur bade forewell to Melo. Today, she remembered her slain husband and two sons.

---

[36] Gift usually in cash made to the bride or bridegroom on the occasion of betrothal or marriage

[37] Sanctified pudding distributed in sikh congregations.

"Had they been alive today. I would not have been lonely like a tree of wilderness."

Bachint Kaur's heart was split in twain

"But Almighty, who can resist your will?" Saying so she left for her house-all alone.

"I am grateful to you O God! You have still been merciful to my abnormal daughter." She was talking to herself as she walked on her way.

"Had you not done even this much, what could I do in that case?" Speaking like this she reached home and collapsed on the cot.

She kept lying there till twilight hour. She had no sense of her own today.

At sunset, the amli reached Santu's house. He had a bottle tucked in the dabb[38]. He seemed to be very happy today. His happiness was evident from the stagger of his gait. He was in a drunken condition. His feet looked hesitant to cooperate with him today and due to intoxication his eyes wore a redness of saffron tinge.

"Oi choote bhai2….." He called out to Santu from the verandah.

"Oi come on amlia!"

"Why will you recognize us now? You have got a beautiful new friend now." He taunted in a friendly way.

"No no, how can I forget you amlia? You are mistaken only."

The amli was awfully under the influence of liquor and swinging on his feet.

Santu brought him in.

"If I release a jet of urine. I can flush out the whole Pakistan." The amli said and shouted a male-goat-like call.

[38] A way of greeting among the Sikhs. This is however a distorted pronunciation. The real word is Sat Sri Akal.

"Why are you making so much noise you fool?" Har Kaur tended to attack him like a bully dog.

"Who's this? Tai? Sasrikal Tai ji Sasrikal! And Tai ji congratulations!"

"Why are you making noise?" The Tai was still emitting sparks from her mouth.

"Tai ji, Sasrikal- Lots of congratulations."

" I have accepted your Sasrikal and congratulations also. But now you go away."

"Go away for nothing? It's a day of celebration. I will go back only after having a drink." Amli insisted.

"Won't you leave your old habits? Go away from here or you will get a beating at my hands."

"Tai, how can I go like this? It's a day of happiness. How can I go like this? You too won't leave your waywardness. You have as small a heart as that of a sparrow. If you had been large-hearted, you would have brought a bottle and placed it here before me saying, "Come on sons, drink it." But Tai you have not changed a bit- not at all." Saying so the amli's finger seemed to reach Har Kaur's mouth.

"Ve, you want to have a shoe-beating from me? Are you fond of such an insult?"

"Yes I am . Come, take off your shoe and beat me. But still I am your child. Now Tai, let it be your shoe and my head. It's a day of joy today. You beat me as much as you like. I am your son Tai ji." Thus speaking, the amli withdrew himself and stood resting against the wall at the backside.

The word 'son' in a way, sprinkled cold water on her inflamed spleen.

"Ve Santu, give him something…."

"Na, Tai Ji, I am not here to take something. See I have brought the bottle myself. It is a happy occasion today. My brother's home

is restored. Tai you beat me as much as you can. I am your son."
Already drunk the amli was playing the same fiddle.

"Who can strike his head against the one like you. Don't know what they eat for talking so much nonsense. The fool has made my temples ache. Ve Santu, come here. Give him water etc. let him take urine."

"Tai you call it urine? It's a gem. Lord Shiva used to have it before going into meditation. It makes you feel easy. People don't buy if for nothing. Tai listen to me today, just try a sip, you won't find anyone but friends in the whole village." The amli was at his mischievous best now.

"Now don't make me lose my temper and give you a thrashing. Cutting jokes with your mother like a blind weaver?" Har kaur too said in a lighter vein now.

"Tai, you claim so much like beating, thrashing and what not but do nothing. It's a happy day today, do something at least. But no, you are simply making empty talk like ministers."

"Ve Santu, put him off by giving water to this badger."

"Hunh badger! Tai even if I come before you as God, still you will beat me with shoes. Tai, where men of gallantry fail, the addicts like me pass."

"Hell with amlis like you. Ve Santu, why are you just looking on?" Now Tai directed her ire towards Santu and made him slip away at once.

"And now listen to me."

"If you drink with this loafer after today, I will tear open your stomach.

"............"

"Do you hear me?"

"O yes my Bebe I have heard it well."

"Now, shall we give our thumb print on a document?" The amlisaid.

Har Kaur went inside without saying any thing.

"Oi, how aggressive she is!"

"Doesn't matter. Let her speak as she likes."

"If someone is to ask her whether you are married or Melo?"

"Any way, keep silent now."

"See, how she sits inside like a gunman. I think she will spoil your game also tonight."

"She won't do any such thing. But you take care not to touch the hornet's nest now."

"Okay, I won't" the amli said and filled his glass up to the brim.

"Pick it up and gulp it down. It's a happy occasion today." Amli said.

"Amlia, Tai will get angry."

"Tai, you think is a police inspector here? Come I give you the cover; you pick it up. You must be on your own; you have to face her for the first time tonight."

Under Santu's cover, Santu gulped down the whole glass. Amli filled it up again.

"Remember one thing as a forecast of the faqir, she will bear a son. Bring him up as a gift from God chhote bhai." Throwing the glassful of liquor down his throat, the amli said.

"   "
....

"And this son of yours will not be an ordinary one. He will be skilled in your occupation by his very birth."

"   "
....

"Such sons are a great support of their parents."

By evening they emptied the bottle. Santu was well under its influence now.

"You come to my house with some or the other excuse. I have another bottle lying at home," the amli said.

"Tai will get annoyed."

"Yaar you have made her a terror for nothing. Tell her that ' I am going to leave amli up to his house." The amli told him the scheme.

"Tai, I am going to leave amli up to his house. I am afraid he may fall somewhere in the way." Santu said.

"Do go with him Beta but come back soon. I am going to help Melo in cooking the food."

"Okay Tai."

Thus overjoyed at the success of their scheme they left.

"I have enough of it lying at home. But don't drink much today."

"You think, I am a child."

"Tai Har Kaur is not bad at heart. But she is a bit quarrelsome. She would never be polite with anybody. You have seen well how Taya, a Wrestler like well-built man had been avoiding any confrontation with her."

"You know amlia! man dreads woman more than a rabid dog."

Both laughed.

"Man is tamed like this only, otherwise he tends to find fault in petty things like preparation of Dal[39].

Santu came back after having two large pegs. It was quite dark and Santu was well under the spell of Bacchus now.

The food was ready.

All of them had their meals.

---

[39] Cooked dish of pulses, lentils etc.

Har Kaur put her charpoy in the verandah.

Santu checked the chains of the cattle well.

"Bebe where are you going? Melo stopped Har Kaur who was going away after laying the beds.

"I am going to my bed in the verandah, beti."

"And who will sleep here near me."

"Santu, beti."

"Hai! Why?"

"Now he is your husband beti."

"Bebe I am very much afraid.

"Beti, husband is not to be afraid of."

".........."

"And I am not very far from you. You should not fear your husband."

Saying this, Har Kaur left.

Melo was lying on her bed quite confused. On one side the mustard-oil lamp was burning. Its flame wavered like her own heart. Melo was looking towards the ceiling of the room in a state of bewilderment.

It was quite silent outside.

In the streets, at times, a stray dog barked and in the Haddarori[40], a vulture was shrieking. Then a peewit disturbed the stillness of night with its noise. Melo's palpitation increased. She covered her face with a khes2.

Santu came in gently.

He closed the heavy door of the room. Melo kept lying as she was, afraid and confused.

---

[40] Place where skeletons of dead animals are collected for further disposal.

He picked up the khes from one side and nestled with Melo. Melo showed no reaction. She lay speechless.

"Husband is not to be afraid of." These words of Bebe Har Kaur were a great support for her. But still some unknown fear permeated her being.

"You are my life and spirit Melo! I can lay down my life for you," saying so Santu took her into his arms. Her limbs trembled and the entire body was drenched with perspiration. Some wave of terror still moved in her being.

"..........." Melo contained herself a little now. Her fear of man vanished. So far she had heard the voices like. "Eat her up, tear her up' from the wolves in human garb. But this Santu! He was talking to her with great love and passion. Her mind at once underwent a change and she looked towards Santu very carefully.

"Melo, you forget all sufferings of your past. Now you are the wife of Santu. Nobody can now touch even your shadow." The very simplistic Santu sat before her like an angel of love. She felt melted towards him. Her predicament dissolved in to peace of mind. The desert of mind became a cool oasis. Santu looked to Melo, her very own.

"I will drink your total agony myself like poison. Melo, you treat me as your shield. The sword of suffering will hit me first before it touches you." Santu was bent over her as he said this. Melo couldn't know when Santu had stripped her naked during this conversation.

Melo had shut her eyes like a pigeon frightened of the cat. She had pressed her lower lip with her teeth and her forehead shone with the beads of perspiration. The burden on her soul had flowed away like a liquid. The psychlone raised with the brutality of man had subsided now. She had become as light as a flower, quite free from all the mess of mind.

When she woke up in the morning, Har Kaur was doing some routine thing in the kitchen and Santu was serving fodder to the cattle.

After the usual early morning ablutions when she came to Har Kaur in the kitchen, the latter noticed an absolute transformation in her personality. She looked as fresh as the one who has woken up after a sound sleep, like the crystal river water and like a rose blossomed in dew.

Har Kaur watched her more intently. The desolation of Melo's eyes was replaced with the shine of a placid hill lake. She had a crimson glow on her face. The body too was nimble rather than lethargic now. In nutshell, her face mirrored the fulfillment of all that she had ever cherished. Har Kaur also experienced a sense of exhilaration to see her metamorphosed like this. She thanked God from the innermost recesses of her heart.

"You could have taken more rest as yet." Har Kaur's joy was limitless today.

"It's okay, Bebe ji. I've had enough of sleep. I am already late in rising," Melo replied. Har Kaur had seen Melo speaking so unhesitantly for the first time today. Earlier, she would simply keep looking at the speaker with blank eyes.

"Come, take tea Melo." Har Kaur placed a saucer full of tea before her.

Melo took tea.

"The water is heated. Take bath if you like."

"No Bebe ji, First let me clean the courtyard." She took the broom and started cleaning the courtyard. Har Kaur looked at her silently-with astonishment.

When Melo started bathing in a corner of the courtyard behind the screen of a standing charpoy, Har Kaur signaled Santu to come.

"Santu you must distribute sweets. Our Melo has recoverd absolutely. I am out of myself with joy."

"……." Santu also felt like shouting with joy. He felt a tickle in his armpits and he felt it hard to control his sense of fulfillment.

"This is what we call God beta."

"........"

"He gives man troubles but shows no miserliness in conferring joys on him as well. Heaps of gratefulness to you my God !" Har Kaur's heart was choked with true devotion.

Har Kaur was Santu's real Tai

As ill-luck would have it, Har Kaur became a widow when she was yet newly married. Gajjan Singh, her husband received a spade injury when he was irrigating the field. Stout and well-built Gajjan did not bother much for the injury. One day, the wound struck by a lightning flash resulted in tetanus. It being an incurable disease, the titanic man passed away on his sick bed.

Har Kaur was pregnant. She bewailed so much on his death that it led to the termination of pregnancy. Har kaur loved her husband very intensely.

When Har Kaur's parents came to attend the Bhog ceremony, they talked about the rehabilitation of Har Kaur. Santu's father was already married. So there was no-question of marrying her to the younger brother as was the tradition. At last when they asked her to go with them, she flatly refused.

"Thanks for coming to console me. But I won't leave my in-laws2

village for that of my parents. I would rather spend my whole life as a widow."

"Foolish daughter ! how will you spend so long a life? Just look at your age. Even the shadows become serpents for a youthful girl. So don't be stupid. Think of some other companion in life." The mother cried in grief for her ill-fated daughter.

"Bebe, you have done, what maximum you could do for me. Now let me remain as I am. Don't just feel miserable and add to my sisery."

"How will you live alone, you fool?"

"Who says I am alone? The whole in-laws' village is mine. Living with you I will get a number of taunts for you."

"You will face the shoe-bashing from your Deoranis[41] and Jethanis[42], what else to you expect?"

"The shoe-bashing from Deoranis or Jethanis is still better than the one I would get from my bhabis[43]. Here I am sitting in my own house. There it will be only the house of brothers and their wives. Had comfort been my destiny, my husband would not have left me like this nor my child would have died before he had seen the light of the day. The sorrows of in-laws are better than the ease of parents' house to me. So Bebe, don't sprinkle salt on my wounds.

Forget about me and go back to your own home. If you ever feel like coming to me off and on, your sweet will. Well if I come to you to ask for something let it be my head and your shoes." Har Kaur had told her parents categorically.

The parents returned frustrated.

The widowed young daughter had stayed back at her in-laws and they could not do anything.

From that day onwards, Har Kaur engaged herself heart and soul in the performance of her duties. She served her parents-in-law day and night. The workers at home were sent outdoors to look after the work in the fields while at home she took upon herself the all-round care of the cattle-heads. All day long she kept herself busy in looking after the cattle, feeding them, bathing them and making them drink water she massaged their horns with mustard oil. The cattle too developed a great love for her. No cattle had ever dismantled its manger not had any of them tried to pull out the tether-post. Also they had never locked horns with each other at night.

After some time the parents had once again come to take her along but Har Kaur had again refused unequivocally.

---

[41] Wife of husband's younger brother.

[42] Wife of husband's elder brother.

[43] Brother's wife.

Throughout her life, what to speak of quarreling with anybody in her parents-in-law family, she had not even spoken aloud. She remained firm on her resoluteness. At times, the memories of Gajjan Singh stung her like a scorpion but she would remember God in such moments.

The wheels of the chariot of Time kept rolling by.

When Santu was born to her deorani, Har Kaur was very happy. She had started enjoying the company of the child, playing with him, fondling him. Besides, she had taken upon herself the responsibility of household chores. The deorani had never shown a frown on her face. She treated Har Kaur as a pious soul.

With the passage of time the parents-in-law also passed away.

Santu grew young, got married and had a son as well. But everybody kept eyeing Har Kaur with honor and grace.

Reeling under the household responsibilities, Santu's parents too had died. But Har Kaur was still very energetic.

Now Har Kaur was Ammaji[44] for the women of the whole village while she was a common Tai to all the youngsters.

Har Kaur had to brave great troubles and tribulations. But nothing could affect her perseverance and fortitude. She was as firm as a mountain . Standing unflinchingly like a light-house.

Melo returned after her bath.

Her face looked more beautiful now. Har Kaur spat away which was a gesture to ward off the evil eye.

After his second round of tea, when Santu was about to leave for the fields, Tai Har Kaur stopped him saying.

"Listen to me before you step out."

"…………" Santu stood listening to her like a docile ox. He tucked his stick under his armpit.

---

[44] A respectful address for the woman aged enough to be your grand mother.

"Don't talk any private things outside the home to others. The ruffians are out only to make fun of you. So keep the 'secrets' of your room only to yourself. And now you get rid of these addicts. You are a householder now. Understand?"

"I get your point, Tai."

"Today, I and Melo will go to Bachint Kaur. She must be worrying. It's quite natural Santu. She is both a daughter and son to her."

"Will you come back by evening?"

"Oh, evening? We are not going there to weave a carpet. We'll come by noon only."

"And my lunch?"

"We'll plan it like this. Melo and Har Kaur will talk to each other and I will pack your lunch from Bachint Kaur's house and bring it to you."

The changed condition of daughter made Bachint Kaur emotional and shed tears of joy. Melo too reciprocated her with the same sentimentality.

"Be brave Bachint Kaur. Thank God for his blessing on Melo."

It was with great effort that the mother and daughter could disengage themselves from each other's embrace.

"Come Melo, you prepare tea. Santu's food also is to be prepared. You talk to each other. I will go to the field with the lunch."

Melo got busy with the kitchen.

"Such a big change Bebe ji?" Bachint Kaur was extremely surprised to notice this total transformation.

"Her mental state became all right within one night." Har Kaur was laughing amidst tears.

"The union of man and woman has been ordained by God since the inception of the world. Where sinful union made her mentally upset, the socially approved union healed her altogether."

"Great are the ways of God, Bebe ji!"

Melo baked chapattis and put before Har Kaur. A dolu[45] almost full of steaming hot tea was also given to her.

"Well, you sit and talk to each other. I am going to the field. The poor Santu must be hungry. Nobody can plough with an empty stomach."

Har Kaur left with Santu's lunch.

Melo and Bachint Kaur got busy in their soul-sharing.

The mother was bursting at the seams to talk to her daughter. On both sides indeed, there was much to share with each other . In the field, amli was sitting with Santu.

"You did something last night or just wasted the time talking of this and that?"

"Don't talk non-sense all the time, amlia." Santu remembered the Tai's sermon. Speaking ill of your own wife today will be to your disadvantage tomorrow.

"I think you must have kept making ha-ha hoo-hoo near the hunt. Should have opened fire also."

"Amlia, don't you have anything else to talk of?" Santu felt irritated.

"Had I known other things then why sould I have asked this? We know this much only. You tell me something and cool down my parched heart."

"Amlia, the bed-room secrets are not shared like this."

"What made you so wise?" The amli chuckled.

"............"

---

[45] A brass or steel pot with a handle to carry it.

"Anyhow, let it be at night. A draught of liquor frees man of all shyness."

"Amlia, Tai is coming to this side with food." Santu said as he saw Har Kaur coming from a distance.

"Is Tai a dynamite stick?" The amli showed boldness outwardly but he was disturbed from within. He was afraid of Har Kaur due to his habit of taking to various kinds of addiction . He would receive a castigation from her due to one or the other aberration.

"Ve, would you let him do some work or not? You the idle bull, let the family men do their work if you are not to do anything." The Tai chastised him immediately as soon as she reached them.

"Tai, you don't keep quarreling all the time. You will never find a saintly man like me." Amli stood hiding behind Santu.

"Had there been 5-7 more 'saints' like you, the world would really have become a paradise," Tai sad sarcastically.

"Tai you kill me with a single stroke of axe-why do you halal me slowly like muslas?"

"You see? I say something else and he goes knowingly the other way!"

"Come on Tai, give us something to eat. I'm feeling very hungry."

"Do eat with pleasure. But do some work also."

"Why Tai, am I to get earrings of gold for my wife by working hard? Orlse make some arrangement for me also as you have done for Santu. Then I will do work also.

"Ve, who will give you his daughter's hand now?"

"Arrange from somewhere else Tai."

"Now you take food like a gentle man and go. Let him do his work."

After serving food to the amli, Tai sent him away. Grumbling, he went his way.

In due course of time, Melo gave birth to a son. The whole village rejoiced over the child-birth.

Har Kaur named the boy as Harpal Singh. Giani Pooran Singh prayed for the well-being and longevity of the boy.

"God has given us back our Pala." Har Kaur said with great joy. She had accepted this as a Divine gift. No voice of protest had risen from the village.

Santu would call Harpal 'Pala'. The old dried wound had enlivened of course but Melo's company had embalmed it.

Har Kaur took great care of Harpal.

He was still a suckling child. Har Kaur would make him lie with her at night. She would daily give him a hot bath and massage his body with oil. She kept talking to him all day long."

"Tai one day you will lose your mind," Amli would say on seeing her talking with Harpal," How does he know what Pashto[46] you are speaking."

"Get lost, shouldn't I share my joys and sorrows with my grandson?" Tai damn cared anything of this sort.

A vexed amli would go away

"Santu, you have spent your time now okay-but you must put your kids on the path of Sikhi[47]," the Giani would say.

"Gyani ji what time we have for Sikhi. I will hand over the kids to you and then it will be up to you to put them on any path you like.

"For the time being the child is under the care of Tai, let's see on which path she puts him." the amli would join with his usual element of wit.

"But take care not to put him on your path at least. Let it be any other path," Said Gurmukh while coming in from outside.

---

[46] A language spoken by the natives of Afghanistan.

[47] sikh praxis

"Amlia, you are not coming under our yoke. We are going to set Gurmukh on the Guru's path this time," the Giani said.

"Giani ji what to do. Your yoke doesn't fit our neck. You will ask us to give up addiction and that we can't."

"Amli can leave his body not his habits," Gurmukh said.

"This is an invaluable reality indeed! What is life without addiction after all? When it kicks, one feels like roaming about in the paradise."

"You better keep your wisdom to yourself."

This time, Giani Pooran Singh made a programme of going to Amritsar on Diwali, in consultation with all.

In the form of a caravan, they reached Amritsar on Diwali. The streets of the city were very clean. The illumination of entire Golden Temple complex looked very fascinating. The recitation of holy Gurbani flowed uninterrupted. It was a very bewitching kind of spectacle. The people were having a sense of fulfillment by taking a dip in the sarovar.

Ram Das sarovar nhate, sab utre paap kamaate" (Man is cleansed of his sins by taking a dip in the sarovar, in the name of Guru Ram Dass) the Giani was singing.

Melo had a bath herself and then made Harpal also take a dip by holding his arms.

"It was decided with Jaagar, Thamman and Hazoor Singh to get together in Harimandir Sahib on Baisakhi and Diwali," the Giani Said to Gurmukh while partaking Langar[48].

"But nobody has reached so far."

"Its such a huge gathering Giani Ji – may be they are very much here somewhere." Santu said.

"That's also absolutely right."

"In the evening, we'll get it announced in the Deewan[49] from the public address system and ask them to come near the stage." Giani had not lost hope.

In the evening, the Giani got it announced in the Deewan about Thamman, Jaagar and Hazoor Singh but to no avail.

The Giani was disappointed.

---

[48] Free community or public kitchen which is an essential feature of a Gurdwara.

[49] Religious congregation.

"The daily household pursuits don't let man leave his home so easily Giani ji, don't be sad," Santu said.

"The routine things are an everyday affair but one should find some time for the purity of soul also. The world should not be too much for us.

They all listened to the Kirtan[50] and other narratives from the Sikh history in the Deewan.

Before the conclusion of Deewan, an announcement was made:

"All of you are very fortunate to have come to Amritsar the abode of the Guru. Tomorrow will be an Amrit-Sanchar[51] session. Whosoever wants to get initiated on the path of the Guru, should come here after taking bath and cleaning the Keshas[52]. The initiated ones will be salvaged from the cycle of birth and death. Gurbani says, 'Sur narmun jan amrit khojte-se amrit gur te paya,' (The nectar which is rare even for the gods, men, sages etc. – We have got it from the Guru. So this is Guru's amrit[53], dear devotees. Only the fortunate ones get it. So come prepared Khalsa ji. The Kakaars[54] will be provided by the Guru's abode."

The Deewan concluded

"Santu what's your idea of amrit-paan[55]," the Giani tested Santu.

"Oh no Giani ji, whatever time I spend in remembering God is enough," Santu averted the issue.

"............." The Giani kept silent.

---

[50] Hymn singing.

[51] Administering amrit i.e. nectar is a part of initiation in to Sikhism.

[52] Unshorn hair esp. on head.

53 Sugary water.

[54] 'K' The tenth Master Guru Gobind Singh ordained 5K's for baptized Sikhs viz. Kesh (unshorn hair), Kangha (comb), Kara (bracelet), Kachhehra (drawers) and Kirpan (sword)

[55] Receiving amrit at the time of initiation ceremony.

"There is so much time for such things Giani ji," Santu said as if to console the disappointed Giani.

"Gurbani says, 'Hum aadmi hain ikk dami' (Our life rests only a single breath). Who can trust tomorrow? The chain of breath can stop anytime."

"………..." Santu became speechless now.

"Gurmukh Singh."

"Yes Giani ji?"

"You come on the Guru's track. Baba Nidhan Singh has been a man of high spirits throughout his life. Till last-breath, he kept his Sikhi intact. Everybody has to die my son-sooner or later-at least make your life meaningful.

"I'm ready Giani ji," Gurmukh said at once.

"That's like a real Sikh."

Thus talking of religion they went asleep.

In the morning Gurmukh Singh was baptized. All of them returned. Adorned with Five K's. Gurmukh Singh looked very nice. The village people praised him for this noble deed.

"You too should have done it," the amli said to Santu at night. They were in the midst of their drink-session.

"Then who would have given you company like this?"

"That is also right."

"But amlia , there is no use of intoxication. In the Guru's abode, the troubled soul cooled down. It was really a great bliss to be there."

"There is no use, I know, but what to do they won't leave you once you fall in their net."

"These are all lame excuses, nothing else."

They kept drinking till late at night, talking of different things.

Gurmukh Singh got married. All the members of her in-laws family including Palo, his wife, were the baptized Sikhs. This matchmaking matured up without much difficulty due to the Giani's efforts.

Both the families were happy with nothing against each other.

"Even the third rate dullards of others get easily married. 'Don't know where God hides Himself when it comes to me," the amli rued and showed resentment against God.

Palo-Gurmukh's wife was very hard working. She would get up early in the morning at four. Having finished with dusting and cleaning, She would take bath and go to the Gurdwara daily. Along with her, Gurmukh also made it a routine to go to the Gurdwara.

The Giani was very happy with them.

He kept showering his blessings on them.

In three years, Palo gave birth to three handsome sons.

Gurmukh Singh and Palo had nothing against God. They had in their hands a Midas touch which could turn even clay into gold. They felt very delighted to see

Gurjit, Hardip and Kuljit. Every sangrand, they would go for a visit to Harimandir Sahib, Amritsar. Sometimes, the Giani also accompanied them. One day, the Giani and Gurmukh were discussing something when Santu came to them. He was very nervous and gasping with breathlessness.

"Oi what's the matter, Santu?"

"Giani Ji; hurry up. Tai is not well."

"............" They also felt non-plussed to hear this.

When they rushed in hurriedly, Tai was breathing very hard.

"What's the problem Tai?" Said Giani while holding her hand.

"My time has come for departure, beta. Melo is pregnant again. Take good care of her. Bachint Kaur herself, is not keeping very good health. Now it's you only, to look after Melo and Santu.

Don't turn your back on them. After I die, hold a Paath for me. I have spent my life alone but I don't want my soul to wander alone. Beta, take Santu also on the path of the Guru………" and Har Kaur breathed her last. She was lying motionless with her eyes closed on the bed as if she were asleep.

Melo wailed,

"To whose care are you leaving me, my Bebe….!"

The wails of Melo pierced the hearts of all.

"Don't cry Melo. Each and every tear becomes a river for the deceased. Remember only the name of Waheguru…..!" the Giani said.

All started reciting Waheguru… Waheguru. The whole village gathered to condole Har Kaur's death.

Har Kaur was cremated.

After having collected the ashes of Har Kaur, Sehaj Paath was held.

After Bhog ceremony on the seventh day, Santu and amli went for the immersion of Har Kaur's ashes.

On their return, they got another news. Melo had given birth to a girl child.

Santu felt very happy to have a daughter.

"Tai departed and daughter arrived!" said Santu. He named the daughter as Joginder Kaur.

Bachint Kaur was there to look after the baby.

"Santu!" one day the Giani called him while just passing by his house.

"Come in Giani Ji, please step in." The Giani came in.

"Be seated, please."

"You know, what Tai had said at the time of her death?"

"………" Santu was silent.

"Fulfill the last wish of your Tai. The last wish is not ignored even by the executioners."

"Tell me Giani ji, when shall I?"

"On Baisakhi."

"Promise."

"And you Melo?"

"I have been ready since long. Only Pala's father was delaying."

"Right, get ready on Baisakhi." The Giani said and left.

"Those who promised to keep company lifelong are running away now." Said amli as he came in the evening.

"Now you are no longer of any use to me."

"Well said," Santu replied.

"Tai gave you her sermon after all while dying."

"My quota of eating and drinking with you is full now.

Enough is enough."

"Well let's sit for today only."

"No, not at all."

"Brother, he has come on the right track with great difficulty. Don't mislead him now. You enjoy yourself the way you like." Melo had spoken for the first time perhaps before the amli.

"Lo, another Tai has emerged now," the amli said with irritation.

"You could escape that Tai amlia but it is very difficult to avoid her," Santu said with a guffaw of laughter.

"Yaar how long shall I live like this? I am losing fast my company."

"You also avoid such bad habits and coming in the way of others or I will give you such a beating......... says, he is losing fast his company."

"I should better go now. The wise holy souls have gathered here." Saying so as a face saving bid, the amli went away

"Amlia you are left alone now-like a tree in the desert. May those of my like live long!" He mumbled as he was going.

On Baisakhi, Giani Pooran Singh went to a Amritsar with his band of devotees. His heartfelt wish was fulfilled. This time seventy persons including Santu and Melo from the village had got initiated. The people were applauding the Giani.

Amli simmered from within.

"Lo the Giani has started considering himself a god." Looking here and there, he would keep talking to himself.

"The people too are treading the beaten track. Someone should ask the fools who has ever seen the next life? Enjoy and make merry here. Next life will be looked after by the Waheguru.

"Do talk to men like us also, sometimes at least. By becoming baptized you have betrayed me, I feel," the amli taunted Santu one day.

"Amlia, our paths are different now. Once you come on my path, we shall be friends once again," Santu said laughingly and went on his way.

"Hunh…" talks of friendship. As if a sinner should want to cleanse himself of all the sins by taking a dip in the water of holy Ganga river. Earlier, he used to gulp down the full bottle of liquor and now has become a saint overnight."

The days, month and years rolled by. The seasons kept changing with their usual momentum.

Gurmukh Singh gave his children education up to fifth standard and made them join the Akhand Kirtani Jatha. It was a sort of institution where they were imparted training in sikh history, Gurbani and weapon-wielding etc.

Every Baisakhi, the Giani would reach Amritsar with a Jatha[56] from the village and return after getting them initiatied in to Sikhism. He was revered well in the Sikh institutions like Durbar Sahib, Damdami Taksal, Akhand Kirtani Jatha etc. The learned people wished to enjoy his company.

On the occasion of every Sangrand, the Giani would recite these lines from the writings of Guru Gobind Singh.

Khalsa mero roop hai khas.

Kalse main hau karo niwas.

Khalsa khas Kahavei soi.

Jaa ke hirde bharm na hoi.

Guru Gobind Singh says: Khalsa[57] is my alter ego. I dwell in the Khalsa. Only he whose heart is free from all illusions is the real Khalsa.

Taking a Jatha every year on the day of Baisakhi had become a regular annual feature with the Giani.

This time, he had to reach there with 25th Jatha.

All the three sons of Gurmukh Singh- Gurjit, Hardip and Kuljit were now fully dexterous in Gurbani and weapon-handling. Gurjit was twenty years old now.

He had learnt the dare-devilry of driving motorbike with blindfolded eyes. He could also hit his target, with the revolver like this. He was an expert hand at Judo and fencing. His comrades would think that with a little bit of training he could fly an aeroplane also. Similarly Hardip and Kuljit were also equally talented. In loose robes they looked very impressive.

Silver-lining had appeared here there in the hair of Gurmukh Singh and Palo but the glow on their faces was intact. Worriless from the side of their sons, they kept themselves engaged in the service of Gurdwara. Sometimes, they would go to see the boys

---

[56] A band of devotees or crusaders in Sikh terminology.

[57] Community or commonwealth of the baptized .

and sometimes the boys would come to see them. Thus, a contact was maintained.

On the other hand, Santu's son had turned out to be good for nothing. He cared a fig for his father. But the daughter Joginder Kaur was very gentle-just like her mother. Santu was very frustrated about his son.

"Don't worry, this age is like this only. You don't worry much about him," Melo would try to console her husband.

"Melo you see, one day he will do such a thing that we shall not be able to face the people."

"Trust in God. He will take care Himself."

"What makes you worry so much, early in the morning? Is everything all right? The Giani had appeared from nowhere.

"What to tell you Giani ji, this spoilt brat has got on our nerves."

"What's the matter? The boys of this age are prone to misdoings. You yourself have come on the right path only recently. Earlier, you have also been doing such unpleasant things that...."

"Giani ji, I am an illiterate man, but he is a collegiate- well educated. If even the college fails to improve him, then only God can save him."

"Don't be so harsh on the youngster son. Everything will be set right in due course of time."

"Anyway, I agree to what you say."

The Giani went away.

Santu went to the field.

In fact, Harpal was a very mischievous kind of boy. Before college, he had changed three schools in the tenth class. First, he was caught smoking bidis in

Guru Nanak Khalsa High School. He did not mend his ways even in the nearby village high school.

One day, the English teacher asked him to write application for fine-remittance. Harpal didn't know the English word 'fine'. So he wrote the Punjabi word 'Jurmana' itself in the application. When the lady teacher read the application, she showed it to the whole class. Harpal felt very small. He pledged to take revenge from the teacher.

Next day, he loosened the brankes of his old bicycle and hit it against the teacher who had alighted from the bus and coming towards the school. The lady fell in to the mud at once. She was helped to be on her feet by the boys of the school. She was made to change her muddy dress with a suit brought from the wife of a teacher living closeby. As a result, Harpal's name was struck off the rolls.

Somehow or the other Harpal was admitted to a third school. Here he shed all scruples and teased a lady teacher. It raised a commotion. Harpal was beaten to the pulp. When it was decided to strike his name off the roll, all the boys came up in his support as they were annoyed with the teacher due to her strict observance of discipline. But the school-staff boycotted him unanimously. No teacher talked to him. Nobody ever asked him to study. Harpal would come to school at his sweet will and then go back majestically.

Prior to the final exams, the ninth class hosted a farewell- feast to the departing tenth class. At the time of group photograph there was again a dispute.

The lady-teacher insisted that they will not sit for photograph if Harpal is allowed to sit in the group. On the other hand the students of tenth class said that if Harpal is left out, all the boys will boycott the photograph.

Altercation ensued for sometime.

With the intervention of the Headmaster, it was decided that both-the teacher and Harpal will not sit for photograph.

The decision was accepted unanimously and the photograph was taken without any disturbances.

Then, after matriculation, Harpal joined D.M. College Moga. His habitual vagabondry continued here also as everywhere else. Therefore, Santu always felt disgusted with him.

This time, Giani Pooran Singh had decided to take thirtieth Jatha on Baisakhi to Amritsar.

"Oi Santu!" One of the supporters of Pooran Singh addressed him by his old name even though following initiation, he had become Santa Singh.

"Yes Giani Ji?" Santu said with great humility.

"This year, very pious personalities are reaching Amritsar on Baisakhi. We shall take as big a jatha as possible."

"Definitely Giani ji."

"One person must go from each family. We have asked Gulwant for truck. We are going to ask Mukhtiar Fauji of Naginder Singh-we shall get it announced from the Gurdwara also you take along Karamjit and others in the morning tomorrow and collect ration."

"Right!"

And the Giani left.

The day of Baisakhi came again on 13 April, 1978. There was a great hustle and bustle in and around Durbar Sahib. The devotees had thronged to Durbar Sahib in thousands. The entire space from Darshani Deodhi to the Prikarma was jampacked. A countless multitude of people was, in a way, cleansing its soul of the dirt of sins by taking a dip or bath in the holy sarovar.

The Manji Sahib Diwan Hall was abuzz with a massive Diwan. The Ragis were regaling the audience by narrating incidents of valour from sikh history.

All of sudden a bad and sad news startled everybody. It disrupted rapt concentration of the listeners. It raised a tumult among the devotees.

The Nirankaris were carrying out a huge procession in the Railway Colony. The marchers were propagating against Sikhism in a very objectionable and provocative language.

It was impudence, not audacity.

The hardliner Sikhs felt infuriated and they took up their weapons for confrontation. But some calm and composed elders succeeded in persuading them. It was decided to settle the issue peacefully. A band of about one hundred fifty Sikhs prayed to Waheguru and set out for the Railway Colony. They were moving ahead chanting Satnam Waheguru through Lohgarh Gate. Gurmukh Singh's son Gurjit was also a part of this group. They were simply going to request the Nirankari chief to stop propagation against Guru Granth Sahib and avoid hurting the sentiments of Sikhs.

They had hardly reached the pandal[58] when a random fire was opened on them. It led to a stampede. Thirteen Sikhs of the group were killed and seventy eight others got seriously injured. A stream of blood could be seen on the spot.

Gurjit Singh Khalsa was also one of the killed thirteen Sikhs. The bullet had hit hard his temple.

The Sikh community as a whole was gripped with a sense of gloom. The people were comparing this incident with the Jallianwala massacre. It had given a severe jolt to Punjab as a whole.

On 14 April, the dead bodies of the deceased were kept in Guru Ram Das Niwas after the postmortem. Next day, they were carried in the shape of procession to Viveksar and cremated. Here one man was killed in encounter with the police.

Apart from all sikh organizations, the heads of sikh sects and saints had also reached on the occasion.

Gurmukh Singh didn't mourn Gurjit's death at all.

---

[58] Shelter erected for public meeting.

"He was given by the Guru and in His service he has laid down his life," he had said. But Palo definitely had wept bitterly at the death of her youthful son. The separation of the son in the prime of his youth, had become an ever-lasting wound for her.

"Bebe ji, why do you lose heart like this?"

"Beta Hardip! You won't ever understand a mother's Heart."

"Maa, let the time come. Don't call me the Guru's Sikh if I don't take revenge from the killers by killing more than they have killed our men." Hardip was hell-bent on taking vengeance.

"..........." The mother kept sobbing only.

"Bebe ji, we are the sons of that Guru who fought seventeen battles but never faced defeat. He sacrificed all his four sons but never showed any sign of sadness. He spent time in the Macchiwara forest, lying on the ground with his head resting on a brick. But still he thanked the Akal Purkh and always remained in high spirits."

"Beta he was a great spiritual Master. But we are underlings of this world only."

"That is why we cannot bear even a thorn-prick. Bebe ji, I would say one thing today, whoever Panth-hater comes before my eyes now, will not go back on his legs. He will be picked up either by the people or carried by the police-truck to the cremation ground. I don't believe in doing excesses on a anybody but if anybody challenges Sikhism now, he will not be spared." Hardip emitted sparks in excitement.

"......." The mother had now contained herself to a great extent.

"Bebe ji! The Guru's small sons sacrificed themselves smilingly but didn't yield to Auranga. That's why the Sarbloh Granth describes Khalsa as the army of God. And Bachittar Natak of the tenth Master says that the aim of religion is to produce the righteous and kill the sinners."

"............"

"My mother! You try to become Mai Bhago and steel your nerves. Let the time come-we must take our rights with the grace of God."

"........."

"Now I would take leave of you Bebe ji. I'm getting late." And Hardip left.

The mother was still sitting gloom-stricken.

The Nirankari shoot-out incident had hurt the Sikh sentiments on one hand and on the other made the collegian Sikh youths think seriously whether Sikhism will be able to maintain its existence. How deep are its roots? From which side does it face threat? How safe is Sikhism today? What are our duties towards the Panth in this state of affairs? etc.

"Je jeewei pat lathi jai, sabh haram jeta kichhu kahi." (If living costs loss of honour, then everything you eat goes waste) Inspired by this Gurbani message, a number of youths abandoned their studies and entered the arena of Dharam-Yudh[59].

Saying a final farewell to their homes, they decided to be a part of 'Do or Die' struggle. They subtracted all comfort from their life. They gave up all addiction and got addicted to their cause only. Also they stopped getting their beards trimmed, listening to film-music and started singing paeans to the Guru,i.e. the great tenth Master who had instilled a new life in an otherwise demoralized nation.

As the colleges became the hubs of activity for various organizations, the government got alert. The police was equipped with more and more powers as well as modern weaponary.

The college boys also stressed collecting weapons somehow or the other. The organizations started spreading their roots far and wide.

Frustrated and disgusted with the Nirankari firing incident, the NRI Sikhs extended their all-out support to the militant

---

[59] A struggle for the protection of faith

organizations. Due to generous financial assistance from abroad, the clandestine supply of modern weapons from across the borders also started. Some youths settled comfortably in other countries also joined the struggle. A wave of heart-rending incidents was let loose in Punjab.

The daredevil yellow motorbike-borne youths would appear all of a sudden from the thin air, sprinkle bullets and then vanish nobody knew where. This was a mystery for all.

The police would raid the colleges and houses to pick up the youths both guilty as well as innocent and beaten up to the extent that they were disabled for life.

No argument, no appeal or lawyer was of any help. The police enjoyed a free hand.

The parents of young boys were living an accursed life. Punjab, was in a way, visited by a genii. Nobody knew when it would be the turn of his or her son.

On Monday, the police picked up Santu's son Harpal alongwith Bitti and Kitti two of his comrades in the afternoon from the college. They tried their best to prove their innocence. But who would listen to them. The police tied the hands of the boys at their back, threw them in the truck and drove away.

There was a tumultuous atmosphere in the college which closed down in protest. The classmates of the picked-up youths informed their parents, prepared news reports and sent them to different newspapers offices.

The Federation workers tried their best for their release but all in vain. Nobody listened to them. When Santu got the news of Harpal's arrest he lost his wits for the time being. Melo, too beat her chest in impotent fury.

Santu reached Giani Pooran Singh without losing anytime.

"Giani Ji, I am ruined. The police has lifted Pala from the college," said Santu and started weeping bitterly.

"But why? Why did they pick him up?"

"This is what is beyond my understanding also. The college boys say that a police truck came, threw the boys in it and drove away."

"Any fault?"

"Don't know Giani ji what revenge this boy is taking from me."

Santu was still weeping.

"Why do you lose heart? Have patience and trust in God. We shall go to the sarpanch and hold the Panchayat. So don't be foolish and be brave.

"Giani ji, although he is not my flesh and blood yet he is very dear to me. Nobody can trust the police these days….. lest they should……."

"Santu losing courage won't do any good. If you keep your spirits intact, then we can do something. So stop it now. Weeping doesn't behove men but you are leaving behind women in shedding tears."

They moved towards the sairpanch.

The day had turned in to dusk.

The pall of darkness was descending fast on the village.

"Sarpanch Sahib, are you in?" The Giani called out to Sarpanch from outside.

"Come in Giani Ji, come in."

The sirpanch was sitting comfortably on his charpoy. He seemed to have taken some extra-large pegs of the country liquor. He had kept his turban on one side, so his semi-bald head glistened like a new brass trough in the pale electric light and his small bun tossed in the middle of his head.

"How are you here at this hour?" he said and the frame of the charpoy squeaked as he moved aside a little.

"What to tell you sarpanch Sahib, the police has taken away Santu's son Harpal." The Giani nodded his head in disappointment.

"When?" Sarpanch's mouth released a whiff of liquor stench as he opened it.

"In the afternoon today itself. Two more boys of the village have also been taken away.

"Why?"

"God knows."

"To which police station they have taken the boys?"

"This also, only God knows."

"Then what is the solution?"

"They have picked them up from Amritsar college. They must be with the Amritsar police, I think." Santu felt very uneasy.

"No it's not necessary. The way, police is empowered in Punjab, the force from any district can go anywhere for lifting the accused."

"………." They became answerless.

"You come tomorrow early in the morning. We shall go to know where the police has taken the boys."

"But sarpanch sahib, in one night's time they will make the boys unable to walk for life." Santu's heart sank at the very imagination of police torture.

"No, it's not that easy. You come to me in the morning. We shall go straight to the D.S.P. Don't worry, go home. They won't even touch the boys." Saying this he twisted the curl of his jute like moustache.

Sad and dejected they came back.

"What's the use of such a sarpanch? You see how he is sitting drunken at home. No sense of responsibility at all!" The Giani said.

"This is how a police tout should behave. The children are rotting somewhere in a police lock-up and the sits bragging at home."

"You go home and console Gurmel Kaur. God will do well. We shall take the sarpanch to police-satation tomorrow morning. We could have gone without him also but nobody will listen to us.

"To home, I am definitely going Giani Ji but I shall not be at peace even there."

"Trust God." And they parted for their respective homes.

Santu went home and found Melo and Joginder Kaur resting scared against the walls. None of them had bothered to light the hearth. Santu fell on the bed with a thud. The whole family was frightened. Nobody was worried about meals. They were awfully worried about Harpal. A sense of extreme uneasiness pervaded the atmosphere.

Late at night the Station House Officer (S.H.O.) Brar ordered Harpal and his associates to be brought out the lock-up. Their faces looked as pale with fear as an autumn leaf. Their throats were dry and the hearts palpitated violently in their chests.

"Well, what do you say?" Brar asked them. His hairy nostrits looked like releasing the breath with great difficulty.

"........." The boys were silent.

"If you tell something straightway, it will be in your interest only." The Head Constable said from one side. He had removed his turban and put it aside. The red phift clung to his forehead like a bride in trousseau[60].

"We know how to extract some information well. Our thrashing makes even the walls speak." The head constable said again. He was suffering from bad cold. That is why he was creating a sound like that of a reed-pipe from his nose again and again.

"Sir, you ask us something at least." Harpal said. He had not been able to understand so far why they were arrested.

"Who are the extremists in your college? Where from do they get the weapons? Who gives them financial aid? Who are those determined to kill the Nirankaris?" The S.H.O. threw many darts of questions in one go. The boys were surprised. They had no answer to any of the questions. They had heard the word 'extremist' for the first time in life. They least knew what it meant."

"..........." They kept silent.

"Think for a while. Don't make entreaties afterwards. I give you fifteen minutes to think over. Then don't say I had not told you. I am gentle with the gentle and butcher with the crooks," the S.H.O. said and left with his retinue.

---

[60] Under-turban band of cloth.

"................" The boys stood perplexed under star-spangled heavens. Blood seemed to have forsaken their faces. What could they tell when they did not know anything? They failed to think what to do. They were being punished for no fault of their own.

"What should we do?" Bitti asked Harpal. He stood perspiring in the stillness of night.

"What can we tell them when we don't know anything?" Harpal too was helpless.

"But we must tell them something," Kitti spoke in utter helplessness.

"If we name someone they will pick him up tomorrow. It will create enmity against us in the college," Harpal said.

"This is unavoidable now. We must choose from either the values of loyalty and police which is at hand."

Bitti was shaken from within his heart.

After fifteen minutes, the S.H.O. appeared like a genii.

All became silent.

"Well, boys! Have you decided something? The S.H.O. asked for their decision.

"Sir, we don't know anything. We have heard the word 'extremist' for the first time from you only," said Harpal.

"Make him lie prostrate on the floor," the S.H.O. ordered. Complying with the order, a constable overpowered Harpal. His cries broke the stillness of the night but they were falling flat against the walls of the police-station.

"Speak now, you fucker of your own sister," the S.H.O. first tried himself. The police-beating had incapacitated Harpal for the time being. The bludgeoning of knuckles had made his whole body generate heat waves.

Bitti and Kitti were greatly terrorised at the sight of Harpal.

"We are already not free from other problems and now these bastards have come up to bother us." Saying this the S.H.O. hit Harpal on his head and felled him like a tree.

Bitti and Kitti were trembling with fear.

"Wait a while. Your turn is yet to come. So far, we have not even touched you and you are trembling without any reason," the Head constable said.

"Throw them in the lock-up. We'll talk to them tomorrow." The S.H.O. ordered the Head Constable and turned towards Kitti and Bitti.

"Think over well till the next night otherwise you will also get such a treatment as may make you fall at my feet."

The S.H.O. threw aside the stick and went away.

The constables threw Harpal and his comrades in to the lock-up as if they were a bundle of bricks, not human beings.

Harpal's groans were audible up to the verandah. The insomniac sentry felt enraged at this and hurled choicest invectives at him.

"Why, you son of fornication! Whom do you want your cries to hear? Since midnight the mother -fucker has been torturing me….. if now you pretend such groan, I will thrust a stick in your…. In colleges, the bastards consider themselves princes and here start crying like women." The sentry at the gate looked very

much disturbed. His heavy boots were crushing the floor. He would have a very wide yawn after short intervals. It was followed with a sound resembling the scream of a beaten dog.

Throughout the night Harpal's groans and abuses of the sentry did not cease.

In the morning next day, the Giani went to the sarpanch's house. The sarpanch was taking tea. Tea was served to the Giani also.

"Giani ji, you reach the bus-stand. I am coming after changing" the sirpanch said.

The Giani left for the bus stand.

The sarpanch's wife came with his clothes.

"I feel like shooting this bloody Giani." The sarpanch gnashed his teeth in exasperation.

"Why? What has he stolen from your house?" The wife said. She was a God-fearing woman.

"Someone should ask him whether I am the sarpanch or he? Whenever something goes wrong in the village, he is on his toes without any sesse at all."

"So what? He thinks of people's welfare only."

"Doesn't matter. Let him fall in to my clutches sometime, then see what I can do."

"His only fault is that he doesn't share a glass of liquor with you. Isn't it?"

"Why no fault? Makes everybody receive amrit. Is he to turn the village into a monastery?"

"Still he puts people on the right path rather than leading them to liquor vend like you."

"You tell me one thing. You are my side or his? You are supporting him as if he is your Devar?"

"I don't support anybody for nothing."

"What else are you doing this?"

"I only call a spade, a spade."

"Don't make me lose my temper I tell you. Are you my wife or his?"

"........" Sarpanch's wife thought it wise to avoid the situation and slipped away from the scene.

Such an eccentricity of behaviour was something very common with the sarpanch. His wife had spent so many years with him like this only. Now even when his sons and daughters were also married off, there was no improvement in his behaviour. When he was irritated over something he would pour all his irritation on to his consort.

The Panchayat reached the police-station.

There were so many people in the premises of police-station.

The Panchayats of different villages had pursued the arrests of many other boys also.

Due to his having a direct nexus with the S.H.O. he went straight to his office.

The S.H.O. and Head Constable were busy in several files.

"After all, you too have shown your face sarpanch! Your visits have become very rare now," said the S.H.O. and shook hands with the sarpanch.

"What to tell you Brar Sahib, there's hardly anytime even for scratching my head."

"How could you find time today then?"

"You know, need takes you anywhere. Election is round the corner you see," the sarpanch told the real thing. He did not believe in talking equivocally with the police inspector. They were very much open with each other.

"What new sops are you promising with the people this time?"

"We are looking for them as yet."

"People are not as much foolish now as they used to be," the Head Constable said.

"Anyway, well do something."

"What brings you here today." The police officer came to the point now. He knew it already that Harpal belonged to the sarpanch's village.

"You know it well. You have lifted a boy from our village." sarpanch was surprised to hear the officer's question.

"What's his name?"

"Harpal."

"What should we do with him?"

"What's his fault?"

"He is a part of the extremist movement."

"He is a loafer type of boy. There is no chance at all of his participation in extremist activities. I thought he must have teased a girl."

"The college where he studies, is a den of extremists." The S.H.O. was using police tactics now.

"Is it….!" sarpanch's mouth remained agape with wonderment.

"Are you sleeping or what? Ever since the Nirankari shoot out, all the Sikh youths have tilted towards terrorism. Now they and the Nirankaris are always daggers drawn at each other. What we are to find out is the source of their deadly weapons."

"………." sarpanch just looked on in utter stupefaction.

"After this Baisakhi day incident, the Sikh boys have started taking nectar of initiation. Whosoever is baptized like this becomes a terrorist straightway."

"Brar! I never knew this. By God, never…."

"Now you have come to know?"

"Yes, I have, but how to console the parents of the boy."

"This is for you to see."

"Can we spare him by extracting something in lieu?"

"Yes, I can do that also. But it is very difficult indeed!"

"Okay, let me talk to them."

"Do it, if you can."

The sarpanch came out.

The whole Panchayet gathered round him at once. Santu was exceedingly crestfallen.

"Giani Ji, the matter is very dangerous here," said the sarpanch and startled everybody.

"At least we should know something?"

"Brar says Harpal mixes up with the extremists. They are out to kill the Nirankaris."

"............." All of them pulled long faces to hear this.

"He is not alone. There are other boys also from his college."

"..........." Silence marked the somberness of the occasion.

"However, I am not convinced with police version but there must be some solution to this, sarpanch sahib!" Giani showed the courage to ask this.

The sarpanch took the Giani and Santu aside.

"The situation has not yet gone out of our hands. Brar is my own man. Should I ask him about some give and take, if you say?

"Sirpanch Sahib, the boy is innocent. We shall do any damn thing in duress but thus harassed by the police, what will the boys do if not pick up weapons? The Giani said.

The sarpanch felt infuriated but observed silence in view of the imminent elections.

"Giani Ji, we'll do something. Let's think of freeing the boy first. Let them not make him unable to walk." Santu's throat was choked with emotion.

"This is for you to see. I won't put you on this path, "the sarpanch pretended to be very honest," So brother you see your own will. Don't say afterwards that sarpanch asked you to pay even a penny.

"How much will work here?" Santu said just to have an assessment of the demand.

"Only Brar knows, or the God above," the sarpanch said raising both his hands skywards.

"Sarpanch just smell something from the inspector."

"That I will do."

"We'll make some or the other arrangement. First let the boy be freed from here." Santu could complete the sentence with great difficulty due to his tear-choked vocal chords.

The sarpanch went to the S.H.O.'s office.

"I don't see a very bright future for the coming generation." said the Giani to Santu.

"............" Santu was silent.

"They say; anger takes man on the path of crime. The innocents are being pushed behind the bars. How long the youth will put up with all this? Santu, our times were different. Today's boys don't get beaten with folded hands. You must remember what I say today."

"..........."

"Santu Gurbani says that you flare up only when the other's arrow hits you. The next generation is not that gentle."

"..........."

The sarpanch was sitting with the police officer in quite a happy mood.

"Brar, release the boy just once. You can pick him up again if you like. I also have to keep my face in the village. The party is ready to pay with folded hands."

"How much will they pay?"

"This you have to tell."

"Ten thousand?"

"It's too much. Just look at the election season yaar. Don't measure all with the same yard."

"Well, let them pay five thousand. It's for your friendship only."

"Right I'll get you five thousand. But listen one thing from me and very carefully. The boy's father would shell out tenthousand also. But the Giani you see, who has come with him? He spoils the whole game. He has got more than half the villagers baptized. Just for nothing. Thinks himself the head of the village. It's only Santu who agrees otherwise he was saying," why pay anything when the boy is innocent."

"Is it........?

"Yes, or course."

"Then I must find time for him also."

"Definitely."

"Remember one thing sarpanch....."

The police officer touched the current issue.

"This Nirankari-Sikh dispute is not going to end so soon. It will set Punjab on fire, you see. Then we shall be in a dire need of Amritdharis[61]. Then he will also be dealt with."

"But, Brar! Don't touch him right now. It will dump all my doing in to the well."

"Don't worry. How long he will avoid? Sooner or later we shall reach him also. What's his name?"

"Pooran Singh."

"What is he?"

"Nothing, Just an idler wandering here and there meaninglessly. Every Baisakhi he takes a group of people to Amritsar and brings them back home baptized. Besides, he does Paath[62] in the Gurdwara. But one thing is there. More than half of the village is after him.

---

[61] The baptized Sikhs.

[62] Recitation of Gurbani

"This is why you are so afraid of him?" The S.H.O. laughed as he said.

"What to do? This is politics."

"Don't worry. Be bold. We'll stop his movement baptizing the people with taking Amrit.

The Sirpanch came to Santu and others.

All of them had fixed their gaze on sarpanch's face.

"Well, how much will be needed?

"No less than five thousand. He was not ready for anything less than ten thousand. It was with great effort that I had to bring him down to five thousand." The sarpanch boasted.

" We'll make the payment tomorrow When will he release the boy?" Santu was very eager to get back his son as early as possible.

"Make payment and take away the boy." The sarpanch told them very clearly.

Santu and the Giani went to the commission-agent's shop. He handed over a sum of five thousand to the sarpanch.

Harpal was released.

Due to police-torture he was not able even to walk properly.

The sarpanch came out to them.

"Now listen," the sarpanch cleared his throat," the inspector says that Harpal is given only one chance. In future he should pay attention to his studies like a gentleman. If you do such a thing again, he will not agree at all. Then don't say I didn't warn you.."

"Sarpanch Sahib, even this the time I had done nothing wrong. We-all the three had done nothing of this sort."

"You had some others also with you."

"There were two more boys. Their parents got them released by paying ten-thousand for each."

"You see now? Hadn't I told you that Brar was not coming down to less than ten thousand?"

"Ha! May God do justice against this in justice.

Where will he carry this sinful earning? Guru Nanak had said, "Hakk paraya Nanaka, us sooar us gai (usurping the right of other is a sinful act; it is eating pig for a mussalman and eating cow for a Hindu). Guru Arjun Dev also says that no amount of wealth can satiate man. It can lead him to regression, not progress."

"Giani ji, nobody listens to such things now. He has even gone to the extent of telling me that very bad times are awaiting Punjab ahead." So ask the boy not to indulge in any activities other tha studies, otherwise I won't be responsible," he said and went on his way.

"Well done sarpanch Sahib well done!"

All the supporters left for the village by boarding a bus.

In the evening the village Sath became a center of discussing Harpal's arrest and release.

"They say the extremists keep visiting the college" The amli said.

"What visiting? they live in the college itself."

"Then why did they pick up Harpal?

"He too must be a part of some nasty game. He is not that much gentle."

"Heard that the police is after newly made amritdharis."

"That's why we are enjoying life like anything. Nobody even calls us," the amli said.

"But yaar, why was Harpal picked up? He is not yet amritdhari."

"So what? His father certainly is, if not he himself. He has become Santa Singh from Santu," the amli's urge for drugs was wavering at the danger-mark.

"You are angry with me because he doesn't give you his company any longer," someone told the truth

"Don't worry Have patience! You turn will also come."

They were as yet talking to each other when Inder Ghaint reached.

"Yaar will you help a little.?"

"What?"

"Yaar, our old ox is not rising up on its legs. We have to make him get up."

"Let it keep sitting if it likes. Have you to get your mother expectant from it by making it get up on its legs," the amli said and everybody burst into laughter to hear this.

"It will eat some fodder from the manger. It doesn't touch it from the big basket. After all it is a son of holy cow, amlia. You yourself have taken your feed of drugpills and are now barking like a dog."

"If this is the thing then come on. It's a noble deed."

All of them besieged the old ox. Someone passed his arms under its belly and some other was holding its tail. The amli was clinging to its neck.

"Come on now. Exert all force," said the amli but in the bid to help the ox stand up, he himself fell with a thud on the ground.

The boys again laughed aloud.

The amli got up with his own strenuous effort.

"In fact, I slipped from the cowdung come on now. Let's try once again," saying so, the amli fell again.

The boys standing closeby found their ribs aching with incessant laughter at amli's second fall.

"Amlia let us do one thing. Let's make you stand up first and then we'll try to help the ox be on its feet," Ghaint said.

"Go to hell then. I'm going. I'm trying to help them and they are making fun of me." Calling them names, the amli went home and layon his bed. His house was near the garbage heaps outside the village.

At about four in the morning, the amli felt a stomachache and went to the garbage mounds for easing himself. The ache was still on. It was perhaps due to over-exertion while trying to help the ox be on its feet.

He was sitting, still massaging his stomach when another old woman came and sat near him. The amli held his breath.

"Who are you?" said the old woman looking towards the amli's face.

The amli kept silent. What could he tell as the old woman in the darkness of wee hours was treating him also as a woman as was evident from her calling him by feminine gender.

"I say, who's this?" The old woman asked again after a short while.

"............" The amli was still silent. Having finished with answering to the call of nature, the amli cleaned himself.

When the woman asked again who she was, the amli, fastening his pyjama replied.

"Ma, I am 'he' not 'she' and walked fast to his home. The old woman became silent how.

Next day, the Giani sent a message to Harpal and called him.

Harpal came at once.

"Anything serious. Giani Ji?"

"Very serious Be seated."

They sat together.

"Did you hear what the sarpanch was saying yesterday?"

"Of course, I had heard him."

"Did you follow anything?"

"No, not at all."

"Beta, the way sarpanch was talking, the police will definitely come to pick you up again."

Harpal perspired from head to foot.

"Santu and Melo love you very much."

"……..." Harpal was listening only.

"If you listen to me, leave the college and go somewhere else."

"But where shall I go Giani Ji? There is no place to go for me?

"Time to come is very bad for Punjab my son. You go to Delhi for your own good."

"Giani ji, what will Bebe and Bapu ji say?"

"I am responsible for that."

"Giani ji, will running away be of some help?

"Beta, the wise man is he who runs away even while he is being beaten. One should not be readily available to the police. Afterwards, there is enough scope for escape."

"Giani ji, may be I am overstepping my shoes in saying…. I feel shy in telling…" Harpal hesitated in laying bare his heart.

"Look Harpal Singh, I am your Taya as well as a friend, a brother and what not. You can open your heart to me." The Giani emboldened the boy to express himself."

"Giani ji, what to tell you and how?"

"You treat me as a friend and speak out. This is a question of your life." The Giani patted his shoulder.

"Then listen to me Giani ji. A girl used to be my classfellow. She abandoned her studies after eleventh class. The father died. She has nobody else in the family except her mother. She loves me very dearly. Her mother also agrees but I am afraid of her father only."

"Where does she live now?"

"She has gone to Delhi with her mother after disposing off their land and house."

"What does she do there?"

"Don't know but her Nanakal family lives in Delhi."

"Well, don't waste any more time now and rush off."

"You don't worry about parents. They are not beyond me.

I will tell them everything."

"Giani ji, when we haven't done anything wrong then why is the police after us?

"This is not for the first time with Sikh community. It has always been like this. The people of India are prone to these things. The government has a tendency to magnify the things. It has a policy to creat conflagration first and raise one or the other issue to garner votes in next elections. Now you will see how they attract the votes of Hindus and Nirankaris by projecting the issue of Sikh militancy. This is dirty politics you won't understand it as yet."

"………"

"You move now. Take food I will meet Santu in the noon tomorrow."

Harpal left.

Giani Pooran Singh's scheme had its abortive end when the police besieged Santu's house at half past four early in the morning. It was a truck full of police force.

Santu responded by removing the latch. He was shocked at the sight of police truck.

"Any service for me Sardar ji?" He asked with great humility.

"No service, you produce the boy," said the sub-inspector very rudely.

"Sardar ji, he has done no crime. He has not even gone to his college since that day."

"We know better than you where he goes and what he does. You only bring him out here."

"…………." Santu stood caught in a fix. Receiving a signal from their officer, the constables threw Santu in the courtyard of the house itself.

Hearing his cries, Santu's daughter Joginder and wife Melo started screaming. As Harpal appeared on the scene after hearing this hue and cry, the constables tied his hands behind his back and threw him in the truck.

The truck drove off raising a cloud of dust.

Everybody stood stunned.

The police raid was so fast that nobody had any time to say something.

"Harpal's Bapu, do something. The butchers have taken away the child." Melo cried while Joginder standing nearby trembled with fear.

"What to do Melo? I can't understand anything?" Santu felt greatly stupefied at all that had happened so suddenly.

"Go to Giani Ji. Only he will find some way out. Hurry up now! My heart is sinking. What should I do? Oh my God!"

Santu rushed off to Giani Pooran Singh.

He was going, rather running through the desolate streets like lunatics. His heart throbbed restlessly but he was reciting Waheguru-Waheguru simultaneously. The noisy sound of his steps disturbed the stillness of night.

"Giani ji………" He slammed the door of his house violently. Due to the graveyard-like-silence pervading the whole atmosphere, his voice had reached the other end of the village.

"Is this Santu?" The Giani asked with raised eyebrows.

"Yes Giani Ji- open the door soon." Santu started weeping. The Giani had inferred from the situation that he had come with some ominous news.

"What's the matter? Why are you so puzzled like this?"

"I am ruined Giani Ji…….." Santu was crying inconsolably.

"Now will you say something or………………? Losing courage like this won't do any good at all." The Giani said and brought him in.

The police has again arrested our Pala.

"When?" The Giani could't believe for the timebeing. At last what he apprehended had taken place.

"They came just a short while before and took him away in a truck.

"………." The Giani was lost in his thoughts.

"Giani ji, do something very soon. We have this only son. And that too has been taken away the butchers. Let them not put out the only lamp of my home."

"Be brave! Don't feel so much disheartened. Let's go to the sarpanch."

The Gurdwara priest had started speaking from the Gurdwara loud speaker.

They quickened their pace and knocked at the sarpanch's door.

"Who's that...?" The sirpanch wife asked after sometime.

"Sister, I am Pooran Singh, the Giani."

"Ve Bakhtaura!" The sarpanchani i.e. sarpanch's wife called out to the farm worker from the room where he lived near the cattle.

"Yes Chachi?"

"I do,....... just a minute."

By the time Bakhtaura opened the outer gate, the sarpanchni shook the sarpanch out of his slumber.

Due to an overdose of booze yesterevening, the Sirpanch was a scattered man. Water oozed from his red-shot eyes.

He felt greatly irritated at the sight of Giani Pooran Singh and Santu.

"The bastards wouldn't let me sleep peacefully." The Sirpanch called them names at heart.

The sarpanchani started preparing tea.

"Sarpanch Sahib, police has taken away Harpal once again."

"So? What can I do?"

"You are the village sarpanch. Fine some solution. The police is torturing the poor innocent boy."

"Moreover, Sirpanch ji, what to speak of going to college, he never did even go outdoors ever since that day. Had he gone out of home, we would have thought that he might have done some wrong," Santu said.

"He can't even walk properly as yet."

"Giani ji the police is enjoying enormous powers these days as I had told you that day that I would not be responsible in future. I had got him released once, now you make your own arrangement.

Tha sarpanch flatly refused.

"Sarpanch ji, the boy is absolutely innocent," Santu rued.

"I agree to it but the police doesn't agree. They see some wrong in the boy. That's why they come to arrest him again and again. Why don't they touch anybody else in the village?"

"..........." They became speechless.

Bakhtaura came with the glasses of tea.

"Bakhtaura! I won't be able to take a single draught of it," Santu said melted in to tears. Bakhtaura had a real feel of Santu's agony but the poor man could do nothing.

"Then sarpanch sahib, you won't help us in any way?" The Giani wanted to be more clear about the sarpanch's intentions.

"Giani ji, why do you want me to say the same things again and again? What little I could do, I have already done. Now there is no use."

"As you wish sarpanch, who can resist the mightly?" Santu said with an anguished soul.

They came back without taking tea. Santu walked, dragging his feet covered with worn out shoes.

"Giani ji, what to do now? I have lost my wits. At home Melo's condition is even worse. What should we do?"

"Let's go to the city. God himself will take care."

They changed their clothes and reached the city by bus. From bus-stand they reached the police station straightway.

Their turn came in the afternoon.

"Brar Sahib Sasrikal." They appeared before the S.H.O. with great humility. The officer looked at them with disdainful eyes but spoke nothing.

"Brar Sahib, we have come for Santa Singh's son Harpal." the Giani said very respectfully with folded hands.

"Which Harpal?" The officer pretended ignorance.

"It's very surprising sir. You have brought him today only early in the morning by picking him up from my home." Santu was surprised at the S.H.O.'s reaction

"Listen to me, we haven't brought any Harpal. We are not idlers like you to keep going to other's homes. Now get lost from here silently otherwise I will throw you behind the bars," the inspector flared up.

They came back, pocketing insult and humiliation.

"O my God!" Santu felt like shrieking aloud," he is befooling us in broad daylight." His heart was bleeding in a way.

"Are you sure, this very police has brought pala?"

"What you are talking Giani Ji? It was this police only. I'm not a child. I have seen Brar with my own eyes. They who are denying even having picked up the boy can't be expected to do good to him."

"I am also of the same view. Come, let's see Bedi the Giani said.

"Who's Bedi?"

"He is a very well-known lawyer, He has the ability to shake the pillars of this police station."

"Let us go then."

"He is amritdhari and a man of truth. I have met him several times in Darbar Sahib. He has pleaded the cases of so many singhs. Age wise, he is thirty only but God has enriched him with a lot of wisdom. He always remains in high spirits."

Santu felt a little solaced.

Walking and talking all the way they reached Bedi's office.

Seeing the Giani, Bedi came out and welcomed him with the Khalsa greeting. Waheguru ji Ka Khalsa Waheguru ji ki Fateh." and a warm embrace.

"Wah Giani ji! What brings you today to the doorstep of this humble servant of yours?" Bedi said with curiosity.

"Man is selfish by nature Bedi Sahib. He never goes anywhere without work."

"What you talk Giani ji! I'm blessed and blessed is the work that makes me meet you today. Please say if I can be of any service to you."

The Giani narrated the whole story.

Bedi became serious to hear this.

"Giani ji, the situation is becoming more and more serious in Punjab day by day. Now the lawyers and law both are fast losing their importance. The Police is becoming more and more high-handed these days. You see, a day will come when the police will not care a fig for the judiciary-what to speak of lawyers."

"Then how will the boy be released?"

"Let me try by going to the police station. But I don't hope they will release him. After the Nirankari incident the police has been ordered by the central government to crush the Sikh movement with an iron hand. The police must take advantage of the situation. Now they will arrest the innocent, book them under fake cases and pave way for their own promotions. Money was already no problem for them. People are ever ready to grease their palms."

"Five thousand they have already taken for the release of this boy."

"You see now? One has to pay out of compulsion and their greed goes on increasing."

"Let's go to the police-station."

Bedi accompanied them.

"What's the name of the boy?'

"Harpal Singh."

"Father's name ?"

"Santa Singh

"When did they pick him?"

"Early in the morning today."

"You stay outside. I am going in to assess the situation. Then we'll see to it.

Bedi went in.

"Come in Bedi Sahib. How are you here today?"

"Brar Sahib, you have arrested a boy Harpal Singh in the morning today."

"Someone had come earlier also to enquire about Harpal Singh. We haven't brought any boy of this name. You can check the lock-ups."

"But Sardar Sahib, his guardians say he is in your custody."

"Let the guardians claim what they like. We are not responsible for what anybody says. If still you have some doubt you can check the lock-ups." Brar replied bluntly.

"Brar Sahib, if there is any charge framed against him do produce him in the court. Let the court decide itself."

"Whom should we produce in the court when we have not brought anybody? You can see Roznamcha (daily diary) if you don't believe me. Munshi.......!"

"Yes Sir?"

"Just show your Roznamcha to Bedi Sahib."

Munshi[63] appeared with the Roznamcha.

But Bedi did not even look at it. He knew well the intentions of the S.H.O.

"Brar Sahib, at least you should remain within the legal framework. Honour the law for the protection of which you have

---

[63] Head constable rank official who works as police station clerk.

taken oath. If even police starts violating the law of the land, who will protect India's constitution then?"

Brar laughed.

"Bedi Sahib, our area of law starts from where your one ends. Now make a habit of looking towards the new sun. See what message the new sun brings?" the officer said sarcastically.

"Your new sun is bound to be dark sir. Something, I am afraid...... the Sikhs are detected by the Sikhs and again it is the Sikhs who shoot down the Sikhs. How long will this fratricidal strife go on?"

"..........." The S.H.O. kept silent.

"Sir, had Dogras not betrayed, who knows how far would have been the boundaries of Sikh regime today. History stands witness to the fact the Sikh community has been damaged by the Sikhs only. Nobody else could do that. Had Pahara Singh not played in to the hands of the English. Shere-e-Punjab would have dominated in the world today."

Bedi came out by saying the truth with all frankness.

Santu and the Giani had their own apprehension as they saw his fallen mien.

"How is it now?"

"The police is out to fulfill its bad intentions."

"Now, then?" Santu's knees started trembling. The beads of perspiration appeared on his forehead.

"Now we have only one way out. Prepare a report and send it to the newspapers. Send telegrams to the governor, police chief and chief-minister. May be something good comes out of it. Otherwise Brar is not the one to come on the track."

They prepared the reports and sent them to the newspaper's offices. Also, they sent telegrams to the governor, police-chief and the chief-minister. The telegrams contained information regarding Harpal's innocence and police denial of the arrest.

Tired and exhausted they came back home.

Before sunset the sarpanch reached the police-station.

"Come on sarpanch."

"The guardians of Harpal had come to me in the morning."

"They had come here also. First they themselves came and then sent their lawyer."

"You lay hands on the Giani. He keeps going to Amritsar and meeting the terrorists." The sarpanch said.

"You talk of the Giani alone, we shall implicate Bedi also. Only, I am on the look out for a chance," the S.H.O. said.

"What? You will arrest the lawyer also?" said sarpanch with his mouth agape like a cavern.

"You just keep watching the ways of God. We are waiting for the new instructions only."

"Take care not to involve a poorman like me. Nobody can trust the police these days."

"We won't touch you at all. But come in and listen to one thing. The police officer took the sarpanch in his office.

"The time coming ahead is very dangerous. Once the new orders arrive, there will be a great upheaval in Punjab. Both the police and terrorists will kill each other. As and when you find anyone with fire burning beneath his feet, do inform me, cash awards will also be announced on their heads."

"All the newly baptized boys have fire under their feet. They spit fire when they speak."

"Anyhow, take care. If you have any service for me, come straightway to me."

"All the youths who take amrit or the nectar of initiation, do it at the guidance of the Giani only. There is one Gurmukh Singh's boy in our village. He lives in Darbar Sahib. He emits only flames from his mouth."

"Any reason? Some special secret?"

"Special secret is this that his elder brother Gurjit was killed by the Nirankaris in Amritsar. Ever since that day, he has been writhing with the pangs of revenge. Remember my words today. He will perpetrate a big killing as and when he finds an opportunity."

"Whose son is this?"

"He is Gurmukh Singh's son."

"His name?"

"Hardip.?"

"Inform me when he comes to the village. He will also be dealt with."

"What about Harpal?"

"Nothing for the time-being."

"Where have you kept him?"

"At some safe place somewhere. We'll use them when the time comes for the same. Sarpanch! These boys are the geese which lay eggs of gold. They will be killed on the day of Id only."

"Do, whatever you like." And the sarpanch got up.

"Sarpanch! Don't forget what I said today."

"Not at all. Don't worry." The sarpanch said and left.

Then started a sequence of state oppression, arrests and police torture. It assumed so brutal proportions that the young boys plunged headlong in to this movement while some others left their homes for safer places.

The number of yellow-motorbike borne youths increased at a fast pace. The murders of Nirankaris and police-officers became very common.

Things came to such a pass now that the youths started roaming about openly with firearms on their vehicles.

The 'fake' encounters augmented the movement still more. The boys preferred to die fighting rather than being killed on a canal bridge by the police in the name of encounter with the police.

At four O'clock in the morning there was a knock at the door of Santu's house. Santu was only half asleep at that time.

"Coming, Pala!" he said and opened the door in bewilderment. He was started to see the police jeep parked outside.

In the wee hours, jeep looked like a military tank to him.

"Yes, what is the matter?" he asked the constables in a confounded state of mind.

"Three boys were killed in police encounter last night near the bricked canal. Go there to identify whether your son is not one of them," said the constable with a muffled face.

"Oi you devils! You had taken him away from home. How was he killed in the encounter?"

"Reach soon."

The jeep returned as fast as it had come. Santu felt stunned. It seemed as if his brain had got benumbed.

Then all of a sudden he hit upon an idea and he rushed towards Giani Pooran Singh's house.

"Giani ji…."

"Coming, Santu."

" Open the door soon."

"What is the matter?" Giani asked immediately as he opened.

"What was feared, has happened after all. The butchers have killed Harpal by carrying him near the bricked canal." Santu wailed.

"How do you know?" The ground slipped from under the Giani's feet. He could not bear the tears of weeping Santu.

"The police had come right now. The constable told that there boys have been killed near the canal. He asked me to go and identify. I'm afraid they have killed our Pala."

"Who knows whether Harpal is one of them or not?" The Giani tried to conceal the truth just to console Santu.

"Giani ji, had it not been true, the police would have come so early in the morning. My heart says that they have done him to death."

They took their bicycles and set out for the bricked canal which was at a distance of fifteen miles form here.

Till the darkness gave way to light in the morning they reached the canal. Surrounded with eucalyptus trees, the canal gave a dreadful spectacle. There was no village within five kilometers of its radius.

At a little distance from the canal bridge, two gypsies and a truck of police were parked. The deadbodies of three boys were encircled by fifteen odd policemen.

At the sight of the Giani and Santu, the policemen talked in whisper to each other. When they came near the deadbodies, Santu almost collapsed with a stagger on one of them saying.

"Giani ji, this is our Pala… our Harpal Singh."

Harpal's chest lay open and his petrified eyes were half open. Blood running from his nose and mouth had congealed.

"Giani ji, the butchers have snatched my old age crutches."

"………"

"They have ruined the evening of my life……… Oh God!" Santu started wailing.

The tears had started dripping and then disappearing into the milky white beard of the Giani.

"Baba make some arrangement to carry the deadbody. The guardians of others are also about to arrive."

"After all, we are not going to take it on the bicycle," the Giani also lost his cool.

"Oi why have you killed him……at least tell me, you sinners!" Santu lamented, "You had brought him from my house. What was his fault after all? Why did you kill my son in the prime of his youth?" Santu was beating the earth with his fists while weeping out in anguish.

The Giani stood stupefied.

"Oi Thanedara[64] for which sin you have taken revenge from me

His mother will faint at the very sight of this dead body which she had nurtured with her own life-blood."

"Baba, if you tried to create a scene like this anymore, you will not even get the deadbody. Take it away at once if you can," the Head Constable said.

"Why? Why won't you give me the deadbody? Are you going to do something more to it?" Santu clenched his fists in fury.

The Giani pressed his shoulder saying.

"Don't scratch the truth like this. Truth is always bitter. Bow your head before the great tenth Master. He will settle the score himself."

The Giani's words in a way, sprinkled cold water on his seething rage.

"Hauldar[65] Sahib! You kindly do one favour to us. You arrange to send the dead body up to the city. From there we shall make our own arrangement," **1. Incharge of the police-station (in common parlance)** the Giani said.

The Hauldar went to the S.H.O. to consult him.

"Load it in gypsy and leave it up to the city. Take care that the deadbody is not taken to the hospital for post-mortem." The officer expressed his apprehension.

---

[64] Incharge of the police-station (in common parlance)

[65] Head constable.

"Then why not leave it up to the village itself.?"

"The villagers may flare up and attack you. How many people we shall throw in the lock up in such a case?" The officer was very clever.

"Then let it be up to the city only. From there they will make their own arrangement."

"We are not bound to do such things."

The Hauldar1 came to them again.

"Come on, we shall take up to the city. Further you make some other arrangement of your own."

They loaded the deadbody and the bicycle in the gypsy and came to the city from there the Giani hired a truck.

When the dead body reached the village, the people where shocked.

Melo lost her wits at the horrendous sight of her youthful son's deadbody. Her world was ruined with this untimely calamity. She was striking her head against the walls. Joginder Kaur, her daughter was swooning again and again.

Santu merely seemed to be a body without a soul. The heart rending wails and lamentations echoed in the whole house.

Harpal's deadbody was bathed. His chest had received full six bullets.

When his mortal remains were consigned to the flames, Melo rushed forward to jump into the pyre. She was overpowered by women with such a briskness as if they knew already that she would do so.

Melo tried her best to disengage herself from the women holding her.

Then she started crying bitterly in a state a helplessness.

The life of Santu and Melo had become a barren island with the sudden demise of Harpal.

Beside relatives, the people from almost the whole village came to console the bereaved family. But the sarpanch did not come even for once. The Giani had been keeping vigil on him for many days.

Gurmukh Singh and his wife Palo would come daily.

"Santu we have no way but to surrender to the will of God. The holy Gurbani says," Apne bhaanei jo chalei bhai vichhur chota khai (He who follows his own will, suffers due to distancing from God.) Gurmukh Singh would say.

The arrival of Gurmukh Singh and Palo was a source of great solace for Santu and Melo.

The ashes were picked up on the third day.

The people of the village jointly organized an Akhand-Paath[66] for peace to the departed soul in the village Gurdwara.

After the Bhog-ceremony[67], the Giani and Santu went to Keeratpur Sahib for the immersion of Santu's ashes. Melo did not feel comfortable in saying farewll even to the last remains of her son.

---

[66] Uninterupted recitation of Gurbani

[67] The last prayers for the peace to the departed soul. Thereafter, the formal condolence is treated as over.

"Palo, may I say so mething to you?" Gurmukh Singh asked his wife.

"Yes?"

"Why not marry off Hardip now?"

"I also wanted to say this to you."

"Why did you hesitate then?"

"Don't know why. Let the daughter-in-law come, bear a child and add charm to the home. Now we both keep sitting like idlers here and there, all alone in the house."

"Yes, that's the fact."

"Anyhow, man is after all patronized by God alone but worldly relations are also indispensable. Had Harpal been married at least the family tree would continue flourishing."

"God has taken away their son and that too in the evening of life. His mother has waned within days, the poorthing!"

"I am going to Giani ji and consult him for the marriage of Hardip."

"First consult the boy also. He may quarrel with you later on, otherwise."

"We shall leave it also on the Giani. He will visit Darbar Sahib as well as bring him along."

"Why don't you go yourself and visit Darbar Sahib also?"

"Okay, we both will go."

"Yes, that will be better."

"Moreover, he is not going to agree without Giani ji's advice. He won't listen to us with that much attention."

Gurmukh Singh left.

He found the Giani sitting under the banyan tree.

"Giani ji, you seem to be in a pensive mood today?"

"Sadness is natural Gurmukh Singh. We have returned from Keeratpur Sahib after immersing Harpal's ashes. Great injustice was done to him."

"There's no doubt about it Giani ji."

"You are coming to me, anything for me to do?"

"Yes Giani ji. After God, we look towards you for any help or support."

"Support is ultimately of God, Gurmukh Singh. Man is just a medium a channel."

"The thing infact, is this Giani Ji that Hardip's mother is very sad ever since Harpal was killed by the police."

"Mother is mother after all. She herself has lost a gem in the form of Gurjit."

"Now she is insistent on tying Hardip in wedding bonds."

"Nothing bad about it. With God's grace the boy is full grown youngman now."

"But Giani ji he is very obstinate. He won't agree to this proposal."

"How can he do so?"

"You come with me. Let's have a feel of his pulse."

"Definite we'll go."

Next morning, they sat in a bus for Amritsar.

The atmosphere in the city was charged with tension.

The murder of a police officer coming out of Darbar Sahib after paying obeisance inside, had shaken the police of this area. The well-known officer was shot down in broad daylight.

The central government had declared this area as the 'disturbed area' and called in central reserve police force (CRPF). The banks and weaponary shops were being looted. Who was doing all this was an intricate question that stared administration in the face. Where did the perpetrator disappear after the crime, was also a mystery.

This area was dominated by the police during daytime and the desperados at night.

The Giani and Gurmukh Singh were also frisked well before entering Darbar Sahib.

They entered the holy precincts.

"The way they humiliate us, was never done even by the English even though they hailed from a foreign land.

".........." Gurmukh remained silent.

"It will have very grave consequences. How long will the community tolerate all this?"

"Nothing good can be expected of them. The youths will be eliminated at a large scale and the community will earn infamy for nothing."

"........"

"The people in the past were the men of cool mind. They issued just statements." Now the government should think well. It's beyond tolerance. It will lead to bad days only." But the new generation believes in 'Do or Die' principle only. You see both the guilty and innocent police officers are being killed."

"Even the police is not doing any the less Giani Ji. See how many innocent boys they have killed."

"It's only the humanity that dies, Gurmukh Singh."

"Yes, that's right."

Thus talking they reached Hardip and his group. Some serious issue was under discussion. Everybody wore a sober face.

Waheguru Ji Ka Khalsa, Waheguru Ji Ki Fateh.

The traditional greeting was exchanged.

They sat at the end of the Jatha somewhere. They could hardly make any head or tail of what was being discussed there.

When the Giani gave a furtive signal to Gurmukh Singh the latter came and put his ear near the former's mouth.

"It's not the time now for talking. Tell him 'Your mother remembers you' We shall talk comfortably at home. Nobody is to let us sit and talk about marriage easily here. So let's go to the village."

"Very right. When they got free a little, we shall tell them and leave."

The meeting concluded somewhere in the noon.

Hardip came to them.

"Let's partake langar, Giani Ji."

They got up and walked towards the Langar-building. They saw hundreads of youths with a particular glow on their faces. The Darbar Sahib complex was teeming with the men with round turbans and long robes. Outside, the C.R.P.F. was keeping an aquiline eye on everybody going in and coming out. They had made their bunkers on the roofs of the houses surrounding Darbar Sahib and their guns were aimed at the sanctum sanctorum itself. The entire complex was breing fortified. The tension-charged atmosphere did not forebode well.

For partaking food they went to the Langar Hall.

"Giani ji, how are you here today?" Hardeep asked.

"I felt like meeting you as are too busy to feel like meeting us," The Giani said just laughingly.

"Your mother remembers you a lot. Do come whenever you find time," said Gurmukh Singh.

"Nothing of the time-crunch like. I will go even tomorrow."

"The parents are parents after all. What, if you have become so much detached." The Giani said with love laced with sarcasm.

Not at all Giani ji. The organization work is so much demanding that you don't find any time all all."

"Is organization bigger than parents?" Gurmukh Singh said in disappointment.

"Both are indispensable Bapu Ji. The parents have brought me in to the world while the organization has provided consciousness, wisdom and intelligence.

"What a wisdom or itelligence is this if the parents keep pining for you and you don't even bother to come and meet them?"

"Bapu ji, you are doing without brother Gurjit also."

"One cannot die with the dead my son. In life you have to do a lot for survival."

"You have digressed from the reality. Anyway take food in the name of Waheguru."

"Waheguru."

Within no time they were finished with their food.

"Well, come tomorrow," said Gurmukh Singh while leaving.

"Definitely, I will come Bapu Ji. But won't you meet Kuljit.?"

"He won't be different from you. He will also talk in your tone only. We shall meet him on Maghi Sangrand."

"Right."

"Come with some message from him." Hardip waved his hand in 'yes.'

They boarded the bus and returned to the village.

"Well, what did he say?" Palo asked with eagerness.

"They were sitting in a meeting nothing could be said there. He will come tomorrow. Then you make him sit near you and then talk to him."

"What kind of meeting?"

"Don't know. Some heated discussion was going on. We couldn't understand anything. Only they know what they are up to."

Palo laughed.

Next day, Hardip came early in the morning. The sarpanch was also standing there in the bus-stand.

"How are you, Hardip Singh? When did you come?

"Just alighted from the bus-sarpanch sahib."

"Will you be staying for some days?"

"Only for tonight."

"Good!"

Hardip came home and the Sirpanch boarded the bus for going to the city.

The Bebe was delighted to see her son. She took him in her tight embrace that gratified her maternal instinct in a big way.

"Beta, don't you ever feel like meeting us?" the Bebe asked him with all the love and affection she had for him.

"Bebe ji, it is a work of this kind that hardly anytime is left for other things.

"Jathedar Sahib when did you come?" Gurmukh Singh coming from outside said satirically.

"I have come right now, Bapu ji. "Hardip said and touched the knees of Gurmukh Singh with respect.

The father blessed him.

"Your Bebe keeps pressing me for your marriage says, at least the daughter –in-law will be here if the son has to remain outdoors?

Hardip and Kuljit addressed their mother sometimes as Bebe and at times as Bi Ji.

"Bapu ji, so long as we donot take revenge for Nirankari episode, don't ask me for marriage. We are getting arms and ammunition freely. Once they fall by our way, we shall see how they escape from us. The Gurbani says that if life means loss of honour, then whatever you eat is meaningless, absurd."

"..........."

"Weapons of many kinds have reached Darbar Sahib. Let's see when the day comes. We are not scared of death. Thousands of selfless soldiers have reached Darbar Sahib. It's heard that police or army will raid the complex."

"Beta will our family tree grow further or not?" Bebe was worried about the family lineage.

"Bebe, the tenth Master had four sons and all the four sacrificed their lives."

"Beta, he was a great Master, but we are the underlings of Kaliyuga."

The mother heaved a long cold sigh.

"Bebe, now should I tell you once for all?" Hardip did not want to keep her in darkness.

"Yes, Beta?"

I have to lay down my life ultimately. You marry off Kuljit if you like." Hardip's decision was followed by a long silence. A meaningful speechlessness.

"But he too cannot be taken for sure. He may agree to marry or not. Earlier, the boys always followed their parents in such things. But now a days they would never budge an inch from their own stand."

Hardeep laughed.

"Bebe, truth is always bitter. I have saddened you by my plainspeak. But one thing I promise persuading Kuljit is my responsibility."

"But will he agree?"

"Why not? At last if he doesn't listen- we shall request the five Piaras1.

Just casually, Giani Pooran Singh also arrived.

"Are you Okay Hardip Singh?

"In cheerful spirits Giani ji."

"Giani Ji he doesn't agree says, marry Kuljit." Bebe told him everything very clearly.

"Hardip is right. Let us marry Kuljit then."

"Giani ji, you have also joined this fool," said Gurmukh Singh.

"Gurmukh, sacrifice is the call of the time. How will his partner lead such a long life without him after he is no more? Dependence on a sinking ship is not only a mistake, it is foolishness as well."

".........."

"Let Hardip remain happy in the will of God. And it is our responsibility to persuade Kuljit, the Giani said and left.

They kept talking till late at night.

So it was decided to marry not Hardip but Kuljit.

Bebe and Bapu had a sense of relief. The anxiousness to have a bride in the house had infused a new life in them.

At the information of the sarpanch, the police besieged the house of Gurmukh Singh. A truck-load of police force was there.

Hardip was arrested and locked up in the police-lock-up.

Bebe and Bapu contained their agonized hearts to some extent.

The Giani and Gurmukh started running around here and there and informed the organization.

With the rise of the day, the lawyer Bedi reached the police station. The S.H.O was irritated at the very sight of him.

"Whenever we arrest some terrorist, this bastard appears from nowhere. Shouldn't we deal with him first?"

The S.H.O. consulted the Munshi.

"You are hundred per cent right. Nobody is going to ask us in such a situation. We must pack him up sometime Just see his moustache...... like the curled horns of a buffalo."

"Remember one thing, if he is not taken care of in time, he will definitely create a big problem for us. Before he becomes a terror for us let us teach him a lesson."

Thus talking they entered the office in a very irritated state of mind.

"Sasrikal Brar Sahib!"

"Sasrikal" The officer replied very rudely

"Yes?" The S.H.O. sat erect on his chair.

"Sir, I have come with a submission to know the charges against Hardip the boy you have arrested today." Bedi asked with great humility.

"Ask this from the court. We are not your servants."

"Brar Sahib! Inquiry will start at your level only."

"You just tell me, have you signed a contract to save all the terrorists?" The S.H.O. talked in a very impolite manner.

"This is my profession Sir." Bedi said and the inspector pursed his lips.

"Now what do you want from us?" The clever munshi wanted to see only one side of the picture.

"Sir either you release him or produce him in the court after necessary inquiry."

"We have brought him today only. When to initiate inquiry and when to produce in the court? Are we meant here for him only? Have we nothing else to do?"

"Please do it tommorw, Sir."

"Yes, we'll do that," the S.H.O. replied at once.

As Bedi got up to leave, the officer stopped him.

"Bedi Sahib, what to speak of enmity people avoid even friendship with the police. So bear it in mind that enmity with police ia always harmful." The S.H.O could not help revealing his real self.

"Brar Sahib, should I take it as a warning or threat?"

"………." The inspector didn't say anything.

"Sir, we are all pursuing some or the other profession. Your duty is to arrest and ours is to help the culprit get released. So why not leave personal grudges and show commitment to our professions only? Brar Sahib, I have all regard for you."

"................"

"Brar Sahib, let us leave personal grievances and be honest to the nation and law of the land. Then all bitterness will be washed out on its own." And Bedi left the police-station.

"See how the bastard talks non-sense. He will not come on the right track unless we teach him a lesson. You call Dhattu at night so that we can clear this thorn off our path," the S.H.O. said to the munshi.

The officer was gnashing his teeth with rage.

At night, he ordered Hardip to be brought out of the lock-up. There was not trace of fear on Hardip's face as he came out.

"Well boy, if you come under our yoke like a gentleman, it will be in your interest only. Otherwise we have no help but to make you lie prostrate," the officer tried to frighten Hardip.

"I have done nothing so far. Why are you trying to frighten me for nothing," Hardip replied very boldly.

"It means, so far you have not done any crime but intend to do?"

"No I don't have any such intentions."

"Then, you won't tell anything?'

"What can I tell? You have not asked anything so far."

"From where do you get weapons?

"You talk of those weapons? Just give me this revolver of yours and then I will see how you get if back or make me admit that I have it." Hardip was not at all afraid.

The S.H.O. was awestruck to hear this. He never expected the boy to speak so bluntly. He took it as a great insult to his authority.

"Then you won't stop short of making us butchers? Is there no way out for you?" The officer was greatly perturbed with anger.

"How can I make so the one who is already a butcher? You have shown no mercy in killing innocents like Harpal. Don't worry the Guru's Singhs are after you. They will settle the scores one day."

"............" The inspector mellowed down now. He had never ever thought that he was also on the hit-list of terrorists.

He stood caught in a fix, quite flabbergasted.

"Sir, your phone," a constable came running and said.

"My phone?"

"Yes, Sir."

"Who's on the line?"

"Don't know says, it's very urgent."

The S.H.O. threw the baton and picked up the phone.

"Hello?" he said.

"Is this Brar? A voice came from the other side.

"Yes, this is Brar," he said and signaled the constable to go outside.

"Do you have any love for your life or not?"

The question hit the officer's mind like a hammer.

"May I know, who is calling?" The ispector's legs started trembling and the whole body perspired.

"I may be anybody, but remember one thing-I am not your friend."

"What do you want? Tell this at least."

The S.H.O. was virtually on his knees before the caller.

"If you even touch Hardip, you are no more," the caller told him without mincing any words.

"If I release him, then?" The officer tried to handle the situation in a pragmatic way.

"Then we have nothing against you."

The telephone call was disconnected.

The officer wiped the moisture of his sweated forehead.

"Whose phone was this?" A startled Brar looked behind as the munshi asked."

"The terrorists."

"What do they say?"

"What to do?" The inspector groped in the darkness

"Sir, release him. The way he speaks, I don't think something will fall to our share in this case. And furtheremore we shall invite the wrath of his supporters."

"Very bad times have come indeed!"

"Of course, otherwise boys like him were no more than tiny insects to us. Now they are out to threaten us." The S.H.O. was sad.

"Had Nirankari shoot out not taken place, we would not have to see this day."

"Untie his ropes."

"Yes, untying will be better lest they should attack the police-station itself."

Hardip was released.

Early next morning the sarpanch reached the police station. He had seen Hardip in the village.

"You have released Hardip?" He sat surprised before the S.H.O.

"Sarpanch ! He has very strong support behind him. So we won't commit this blunder again.

"Is it?" The S.H.O.'s words surprised him still more.

"You keep track of some other terrorist. Now we shall keep the arrest quite secret."

"Exactly. The arrest of Hardip has just proved a futile exercise."

"If you believe me, arrest the Giani and explore him well. You will get a lot of information from him. He is the patron of these terrorists. Almost all of them keep coming to him and he too keeps regular liaison with them."

"Wait for a while sarpanch! Everything has its time. We shall involve all, don't worry."

"Keep the action against Giani Pooran Singh secret. He will deliver a lot of information."

"Don't worry. This is our job now. Let the time come."

sarpanch left.

"He has his own grudges against the Giani." The munshi said to the S.H.O. after the departure of sarpanch.

"The Giani does nothing against him. The problem is that he doesn't let anybody vote for Congress. And the sarpanch is a committed Congressman."

"But Sir, one thing you must bother……. If you are to pick up the Giani, you will have to be having very solid reasons for that. Arresting him will create a great public resentment."

"You don't worry. I will arrest him only with the orders of higher authorities. But the action has to be kept a secret."

Thus they kept talking to each other.

After some days, Kuljit's marriage was fixed.

Five men went as marriage party and came back with the bride. It was a very simple marriage. There was no fanfare, no give and take of dowry etc. Guramrit, the bride was an educated and amritdhari girl. She was called Bunty in the family. It was her nickname.

Bunty was a very wise and well-disciplined girl from a very nice and gentle family. Kuljit's parents were very happy to have such a noble and docile daughter-in-law. Her way of dressing was also very simple.

According to the orders of the out fit, Kuljit started living at home.

Bunty would never let her mother-in-law go to the kitchen for cooking or any other allied work. She did everything herself. The whole family was very happy.

One day the Giani came, very sad and dismayed

"Gurmukh Singh, you heard anything?"

"No Giani ji, is everything all right?"

"Bedi, the lawyer is killed."

"When, where and how?" Gurmukh Singh felt earth slipping from under his feet as he asked all this in the same breath.

"He was going to Hazoor Sahib in a bus. He was accompanied with his wife and a seven-year old son. Heard, that they were made to get down from the bus and shot dead."

"Ah! Let heavens fall on you. What wrong had the child done to you. Who killed him, is any thing clear?"

"I have all my doubt on police. He had none against him otherwise. He had nothing against police also but he pleaded the cases of singhs. So I am sure the police have got him eliminated through their own men."

"You see Giani ji, what will be the fate of common man if even the lawyers are not safe at their hands? Only God is the saviour of people like us then."

"God is the saviour of all. Will you go at his cremation tomorrow?'

"Definitely. Nothing to ask in it. Let us tell Kuljit also. He often used to come to him."

"Yes, tell him also."

When he told, Kuljit started seething with rage. His eyes started emitting sparks.

"This is all Brar's doing Bapu. He had threatened him once or twice-Bedi himself told me." Kuljit recalled something.

"Kuljit Bunty is expectant Beta. You must control yourself. Don't go anywhere leaving her in this state." Bebe advised him.

"Moreover, there are so many people at Bedi's support The poorthing lost his life for no fault of his." The Giani also understood the real story.

"We'll go to attend his cremation tomorrow. You look after the cattle alongwith the farm worker." Gurmukh also took advantage of the situation and said before Kuljit could say anything.

Kuljit could not sleep throughout the night.

He kept tossing in his bed. Bedi and his own slain brother had awfully occupied his mind. He was shocked at such a tragic end of a lively and honest man. The killers were unscrupulous enough not to spare even his seven-year child. Just because he pleaded the case of singhs? Because, his work was contrary to that of the police?

Such honest and ready to sacrifice men do not come again and again on this earth. Such a learned lawyer! And they eliminated him in minutes. What was thefault of his innocent child, his wife?

Really, he could not have a nap and spent the whole night waking.

He went to his fields early in the morning.

The Giani and Gurmukh Singh boarded the first bus for the city to attend the cremation ceremony of the deceased.

The atmosphere in the city was charged with tension.

The advocates were on strike today.

It was by and large a curfew-like situation.

The C.R.P.F. was patrolling on the roads.

It was a gathering of thousands who had come to pay homage to Bedi and his family. The situation was tense but under the hawkish vigil of C.I.D. Even the twitching of eyes was not going unnoticed.

When the pyres were ready to be lit, the speakers from various walks of life paid tributes to the departed souls.

The Giani demanded a compensation of 5 lac rupees as ex-gratia grant by the government for the bereaved parents of the slain lawyer, during his speech. He also demanded immediate arrest of the killers.

When the pyres were lit, the supporters of Bedi raised slogans.

Gurdev Singh Bedi- Amar Rahe (Be immortal)

Bedi's Killers-Murdabad (Let them go to the graves).

Hang the killers

Bole so Nihal- Sat Siri Akal

(Whosoever says Sat Siri Akal i.e. God is eternal, is Blissful).

In the midst of slogans rending the atmosphere, the people marched towards Darbar Sahib C.R.P.F. was also walking along. But no untoward incident had happened.

An Akhand Paath was held at Guru Nanak Niwas to say last prayers for the peace of departed souls.

On the fifth day, the police-inspector Brar was attacked as he was coming out of the police-station.

Two youngmen attired in robes and riding on yellow bikes came and fired at him.

The seriously injured inspector came back to the police-station and collapsed. The youths fled with the nimbleness of a hound.

It created a tumult in the police station.

The S.H.O. was immediately admitted to the hospital where the doctors saved him. His family was also informed.

The doctor's extracted eight bullets from Brar's body. Now there was no threat to his life, according to them. But he still needed enough time to get healed properly.

Senior police officers were pouring into enquire about Brar's well-being. Tall claims were being made. Much of bragging was being made.

The newspapers communicated this news to every nook and corner of the city.

The people were wonderstruck at this daredevilry.

Brar was replaced with a new sub-inspector Jang Singh.

Jang Singh was a butcher kind of cop. He was promoted to this position from the rank of Hauldar.

Jang Singh was a very clever and shrewd officer. Immediately after taking over the charge he called all the panchayats to have a cursory glance over the situation, felt the pulse of village elders, heard some complaints and issued some directions as well.

Among all the Panchayats, Jang Singh developed a liking for the sarpanch of Giani Pooran Singh's village. The unity of thoughts made them look eye to eye at each other. And this is what developed between them a chord of 'friendship.'

That very evening the S.H.O. called the sarpanch by sending him a message. The sarpanch appeared at once.

Jang Singh welcome the sarpanch with an embrace. Rubbing with the power-equipped uniform filled him with abundant warmth.

Jang Singh took him aside.

"Your name?" The sub-inspector asked him with a great sense of belongingness.

"Sir, Jaggar Singh"

"Be comfortable first and stop being formal by saying 'Sir' etc. From today onwards we are fast friends.

"................" The sarpanch felt a tickle in his whole being at such a fine display of love and affection.

"From today, you can address me by name. I am very sincere in friendship. You kill a man and come to me. Nobody can do any harm to you."

"............" The sarpanch felt still more elated."

"Shall I bring a bottle from the market to celebrate the first day of our friendship?"

"Why do you put me to shame at my own place? Come , let's go upstairs and sit in the attic. I have all the arrangement there. I am not just a taker like other policemen. I am the one who can lay down his life for his friend."

The sub-inspector and the sarpanch-both went upstairs.

The sub-isnpector took out the bottle of Redknight whisky. The sarpanch was delighted to see the English drink. He passed his tongue over his lips especially by removing his fox-tail kind of moustaches with his palm. Like that of a snake sarpanch's tongue went back into his mouth as fast as it had come out.

"Come on sarpanch! Take this first peg in the name of our true friendship."

Both of them emptied their glasses in one go.

The liquor had gone down into the stomach as if leaving a meteoric trace in the throat.

The first large dose had brought a peculiar glimmer in their eyes.

"Sarpanch, now what to conceal from a friend like you, Brar seems to me a fool," the S.H.O. said and looked at sarpanch to read the reaction of his words from his face.

"No no, Jang Singh he was not foolish. However, he was a bit lethargic. I tried my best to persuade him for nabbing the Giani of our village and even said that it will lead to track down many terrorists. But he didn't pay any attention. The Giani is a devout supporter of the terrorists. What could I do? He kept putting it off. Any they did what they were up to as and when he found the chance."

"Who is this Giani?"

"He is a refugee from Pakistan. He has launched a compaign to baptize everybody. He frequently goes to Amritsar which you know is a hub of terrorists. So many of them keep coming to him."

"What does he do?" asked the S.H.O. pouring whisky into the glasses.

"He is allotted about nine acres of land. He gives it for farming on contract basis. In addition he works in the village Gurdwara, reciting Gurbani Paath etc. Keeps instigating the boys saying." Amrit Chhako-Guruwale Bano" (Take amrit and come on the Guru's track). What else would an idler do."

"Any supprt at his back?"

"Nothing but the youngsters. But the village people also love the knave from heart." The sarpanch could not help speaking truth.

They emptied the glasses.

"Sarpanch. I tell you truly. I need such men by all means. If they get tamed easily well and good, otherwise I have my own means also."

"Listen one thing, Jang Singh, from me also. He is not the one to be bridled so easily." The sarpanch said with full confidence.

"What you talk sarpanch! I have risen to this position from Hauldar rank by setting right such crooks only. When we use our police methods of interrogation the most crooked ones get straight like a yard. I am here and you are also here. You will see how he is straightened."

"I had got another boy arrested. He did nothing and released him soon thereafter. Said, he had very big support behind him. Really, he is very cowardly kind of a man."

"What was the charge against him?"

"I won't tell a lie, there was no charge against him. But he is member of some terrorist organization."

"Where is he now?"

"God knows, but I am sure he lives most of the time in Amritsar only. And Jang Singh, you know, such people don't have only one place to stick to. Wherever they find food to eat they stop there. Famished at home, these loafers take shelter in terrorism. I think all of them are those who were pushed out of their homes."

"These-like are the men sarpanch, we need very urgently. It's due to them only that the next promotion will fall to my share."

"Really....?"

"Of course, government will offer something only on the basis of how many of them we eliminate."

"If my friend gets promotion, what else do I need? You tell me what I can do for you. I won't ever show my back?"

"Then listen to me carefully. From today onwards you have to get the terrorists captured. In turn I will get you award announced on their heads from the government. Now you tell if I can do something more for you."

"Something more, Jang Singh, is that I need a weapon license."

"As many licenses as you need. So long as the license is not made you can keep weapon without license also. Nothing to worry. I am with you."

"I am afraid lest unlicensed weapon should cause some problem.

"Sarpanch! You are my fast friend now. No problem till I am here. I have told your earlier also that I am not one of the opportunist police officers."

"I thought government is making more and more strict laws everyday."

"Law is for the people, it's not for you. So rest assured."

"Okay then why should I worry when you are here?"

They opened another bottle now.

"You come tomorrow morning and give your application to me. You will have the license within a week."

"Right I will come tomorrow with the application duly typed from the courts."

"That's your job."

"Should I have license for revolver or rifle.

"This is also your own choice. All options are open from my side."

They kept talking till late night hours. Even two bottles had failed to make them unstable.

The Giani's arrest kept delaying for one reason or the other. Actually, the S.H.O. wanted to lay hands on him with a sound footing. For this he needed solid evidence against the Giani as also the confidence of his seniors.

That is why time was passing. Jang Singh was a very seasoned officer. It was not his nature to do anything that may turn abortive in the end.

Kuljit's wife Bunty gave birth to a son. It filled the atmosphere in the house with joy.

After some days, they paid obeisance as thanksgiving in the village Gurdwara and distributed Degh (Sanctified Pudding) to the devotees.

The Giani had the first initial of the boy's name from the holy scripture. It came out to be 'K' and the child was named Kulbir Singh. Bebe and Bapu Ji called him Kulbir while Kuljit and Bunty called him Teetu.

The milky white child was very beautiful. He neither wept nor insisted. Bebe kept lost in playing with the grandson. She had no longer anything against the Waheguru. She was very grateful to him.

Gurmukh Singh also loved Kulbir very dearly and kept fondling him in his lap. Teetu too reciprocated it with his charming smiles. The child would keep the whole family engaged.

One morning Giani Pooran Singh was arrested by the police. The police-raid was conducted so early in the morning that the people were amazed.

He was captured in the ambrosial hour. His hands were tied with his own turban before he was thrown in the truck.

The truck left.

"What was the Giani's crime?" The people had their own conjectures. They were groping in the darkness.

As the news regarding Giani Pooran Singh's arrest reached Gurmukh Singh, he gathered the village Panchayat at the sun-rise.

The people had gathered in the Sath.

"Giani ji had never killed even an ant. Why did the police pick him up?" Gurmukh Singh touched the issue.

"Moreover, he is an aged man."

"Nobody ever heard him speaking ill of others."

"What to talk of speaking ill, he has changed the very spirit of the village."

"No other village has as many amritdhari boys as our village. Otherwise in other villages, we see youngmen fallen in the ditches due to addiction."

"The Giani has reformed the village as best as he could."

"Come, let's go to the police-station and enquire about him."

"Yes, let's not lose heart."

"It's our duty to get to know what actually was the reason?"

A commotion pervaded the atmosphere.

Only the sarpanch sat listening in a carefree manner.

"Sarpanch sahib! Why don't you say anything?"

"In which toughts are you lost?"

"The police has captured the respectable man of the village without any fault of his."

The sarpanch got up and said,

"Listen to me brothers," he waved his hand in the air to silence the gathering and continued, " The police is not stupid to have arrested a reputed man without any fault of his." Due to not having taken any intoxication so far, his voice had grown hoarse.

"Lo, brothers ! Listen to him also."

"Can you expect any support from such a person?"

"Nobody can hope for anything good from him."

"He is a man of the police. How can he speak in our favour?"

"He is a police tout."

"A perfect sycophant."

"That is why the police has given him weapon license."

"The others' weapons have been deposited in the police station and he is given the license."

A din prevailed over the sarpanch's comments.

The sarpanch found himself caught badly in an atmosphere quite hostile towards him.

So he had the volte face.

"Oi you, the people of my own village! I am not a man of the police. Who has made me the sarpanch you or the police?"

"We, of course."

"Then, why shall I favour police? If you say, I can swear in the Gurdwara or touch the tail of holy cow. But please don't misunderstand me."

"………………." A silence prevailed all round.

"You kill me if your like but don't misunderstand me please. So far as the revolver is concerned, the fact is that terrorist killings have become very common in the villages today. If somebody from the village comes under attack, we can fire at least one or two rounds. Anything else?"

"…………." All became silent as if they were unconscious.

"Why shall I stand by the police rather than my own brothers?"

"Then what should we do in the Giani's case." Gurmukh Singh touched the issue once again.

"Come, let's go to the police-station and enquire about him." All the men got up as the sarpanch said this.

"No no, it will become an unwieldy gathering. Only five-seven men will be enough," Gurmukh Singh said.

Convinced with Gurmukh Singh, the half of the men sat down.

Five-seven men from the village reached the police-station alongwith sarpanch. The sarpanch gave Jang Singh the S.H.O. a mysterious signal. The crafty police-officer understood it at once.

He did not care for them till noon and kept himself busy with some other things.

After lunch, he called the Panchayat.

"Well, gentlemen! What brings you here?" The officer asked the Panchayat in a slant manner.

"Sir, we have come after Giani Pooran Singh. Sarpanch said. He did not want his friendship with the S.H.O. to be revealed.

"Look, sarpanch sahib! We have brought him on the basis of confirmed report. After preliminary inquiry today, he will be released tomorrow. We are not fond of capturing the innocents. We are also answerable to our senior officers and family-men like you. We too have to bring up our children, gentlemen!" The S.H.O. pacified everybody.

"What is the charge against him?"

"Sarpanch sahib, we too have our own secrecies. So please don't try to peer into them."

"But still, we must know something."

"Please try to understand my position. I have orders from above not to leak any official secrecy. Do you have some Gurmukh Singh in your village." The S.H.O. changed the track at once.

"Here he is What's the matter?"

"Gurmukh Singh we have reports against both of your sons that they are linked to the terrorists. You see my generosity that I have not tried to lay hands on them so far."

"I can't say anything about the elder one but the younger lives at home only after his marriage. Now he has a son also. He has never gone outdoors," Gurmukh clarified.

"No no, I'm talking just casually that we never touch anybody just on the basis of our daily diary reports. You rest assured. The old gentleman will be let off tomorrow as and when the boss comes."

"Sir, if you release him now, we shall produce him when the boss comes." The sarpanch played the trick worthy of pimps.

"How does it matter? He is as comfortable here as he will be with you in the village. So why do you put me to shame?'

"As you wish sir. Who can resist the government?" The sarpanch said.

"Really had it been in my competency. I would have done as you wish. But I have my own compulsions please say, would you have a cup of tea?"

"No, thanks."

And the Panchayat came back.

"Now you have seen how close I am to the police? It's all before you." The sarpanch was happy from both sides. He had got the Giani arrested and was innocent in the eyes the village as well.

"Who can kill a python like me. I can drink ocean without a belch. I can flush out the whole village with a jet of my urine. How will these people match me after all!" The sarpanch had gulped down many larges immediately after the sunset.

"O you man of God! You should not go against the innocent. The Gurbani say, "Nirvaire sang vair kamaida, ghar apne lukilai." (animosity against the innocent means setting your own house ablaze)," said sarpanch's wife.

"You keep your philosophy to yourself only," said the sarpanch. His wife became silent now. She heaved a cold sigh.

At nine post meridian, the Giani was fastened in the stocks. Nothing had been asked from him. And nothing was told to him as well.

The Giani too didn't feel like raising any hue and cry. Due to fastening in the stocks a whirlwind of pain rose to his mind.

The devout Giani attached himself at a spiritual level with the martyrs of Sikh history. In the realm of thoughts, he touched the feel of the fifth Master Guru Arjun Dev sitting on a hot plate. He found himself one with Baba Deep Singh who had kept fighting against the enemy even after he was beheaded. The Gurbani escaped his lips intermittently.

After full two hours, the police officer ordered the Giani to be freed from the stocks The Giani fell supine on the floor immediately thereafter. His aged body had stiffened like wood. He was breathing hard but still he repeated 'Waheguru….. Waheguru' His turban had slipped off his head and the hair had scattered loose. He was not even in a position to tie his hair.

"Hunh…. Giani, now you have come to your senses or not?" The baton revolved in his hand as he said.

"I think time has passed for our talking to each other with love and respect." The Giani mustered courage and said.

"You are free to speak as you like."

"What do you want from me?"

"We want information about terrorists. If you give it to us gently, good; otherwise you have already seen the trailor. We are going soft on you because of your age. Rest depends on you." The inspector said all this in one breath.

"I don't know anything about the terrorists. What can I tell you?"

"Baba, why are you up to becoming our enemy and your own? Tell us whatever you know." The munshi tried to bring him round with politeness. The pointed ends of his lizard-tail moustaches nearly touched his eyes.

"Youngman these hair have not greyed in the sun only. They indicate my experience of life."

"Baba, you think well of yourself. Don't howl like a jackal later on. We shall give you this very treatment daily."

"Do whatever you like, but I won't tell a lie. And also don't threaten me with death. Chinta ta ki keejiya jo anhoni hoi, eh maarg sansar ko, Nanak thir nahi koi (One should worry only that which is not destined. Guru Nanak says that in this world nobody has ever been eternal)." We have come to this world only after our exit was ordained, my dear."

The Giani was once again fastened in the stocks. Nobody was allowed to offer him even a glass of water.

The S.H.O. rang up the Dy. S.P. Someone picked it from the other end after the second bell only.

"Well this is sub-inspector Jang Singh here. Give it to the Dy. S.P. Sahib please. It's urgent."

"Yes, say Jang Singh?"

"An old man has been captured sir, on the basis of very strong information. He is reported to have links with the terrorists. What should we do with him sir. Neither he has done any incident of criminal nature nor is he expected to do such a thing. We picked him only after knowing about his relations with the terrorists."

"You do one thing."

"Sir?"

"Let him off for the time being. Deploy our intelligence men after him to know where he goes, whom he meets and what kind of things they talk about."

"Yes sir."

"The oldman is not going to deliver us anything. So don't keep your eye on making arrests only. Use a bit of technique also. Understand?"

"Yes Sir."

The phones were disconnected.

"Remove the Giani from the stocks and serve him tea, water etc." The sub-inspector ordered and a constable was sent to him with strict directions.

The Giani was freed from the stocks and was made to lie on a cot with a sheet to cover himself. The Giani still did not tell them anything. He was a God-fearing man.

The sarpanch came with the sun-rise

"How was I remembered today?" Sitting before the police-officer, he said

"Listen to me carefully." The S.H.O. patted sarpanch's thigh as he said this.

"Say?"

"My seniors say that this old man is not going to tell us anything. So release him but keep vigil on him where he goes, what he does, whom he meets?"

"Anything else?'

"Then we shall book him on a sound footing only."

"Then why have you called me?"

"By faith! Sarpanch you have said a very childish thing now."

"........." The sarpanch laughed.

"Boss is a very seasoned man. He is a very far sighted man. You do one thing."

"Yes?"

"You take him from here and take credit for getting him released. You will become a hero in the village in no time. Develop your ties with him and dig out the secrets. Nobody will doubt you. We shall be benefited both ways understand?'

"Right! But I have told the people that we have no friendly relations."

"Don't worry, we won't let it be known."

When the sarpanch went near the Giani, he found him sitting shrunk in a corner. But due to taking a little of refreshment and warmth of sunshine, he was able to contain himself.

"Are you okay Giani ji?'

"What okay sarpanch Sahib. The rascals have put me in the stocks without any of my fault. Each and every joint of my body is displaced. Then somehow they pitied and gave me bed to lie on at midnight."

The sarpanch relished a sadistic pleasure to see this pitiable condition of Giani Pooran Singh who had been irking him for long.

"But yesterday they said, just formal inquiry was to be made."

"That they have done. What could they draw out of me? All the bones of my body are aching now."

"Come on, I have come to take you home from here. I couldn't sleep the whole night and set out for the city early in the morning.

I have not brought even any Panchayat member along so as not to get late. Now get up, let us go."

"Anyway, let's go if they have allowed. Hai!" The Giani groaned with pain and got up on his feet. The old bones were aching badly.

Nobody talked or spoke to them as they walked out of the police-station.

Stopping at a tea-shop outside the police-station. The Sirpanch himself had tea but made the Giani drink hot milk. Now the Giani's eyes opened properly and his whole body was filled with a warmth.

They boarded a bus and came to the village.

The news of Giani Pooran Singh's release with the efforts of the sarpanch became talk of the village.

All the people were amazed at this.

"Sarpanch sahib! Throughout your age, you have only this noble deed that goes to your credit," the sarpanch's wife complimented her husband.

"You have always treated me as good-for-nothing. Darling, I don't believe in saying much and doing nothing. Now see how I have brought him home within a day."

"Thank God! You too have come on the right track. Well done!"

"Are you giving me a drink then with your own soft hands?"

"You do at least one noble deed everyday and I will give you a drink everyday with my own hands."

"Just a drink or something beyond that also?" The sarpanch said and pressed his left eye mischievously.

"Shame on you! Now you have grown old with sons and daughters."

"From which side I look old to you? It's only you who have surrendered. I'm still healthy enough. You can try me at night today."

Thus they kept talking to each other in a vivacious mood.

But nobody was aware of the dishonesty and mal-in-tentions of the sarpanch.

In about a couple of years, the Giani had been picked up several times but the police could extract nothing out of him in the name of information.

The Giani was a simplistic God-fearing man. What could police get out of him? He would bear the police torture on his frail body with the remembrance of Waheguru on his lips. His only fault was that he weaned the boys away from addiction and motivated them to take amrit. Secondly, he frequently visited Amritsar. There was nothing else against him.

At the time to last arrest and release, the police-officer had cautioned him saying.

"Well, Baba you must come well-prepared when you are nabbed again. We shall do our final justice to you. We feel ashamed in running after you daily. Are we idlers or meant for you alone? You are not parting with any information and you alone have become a constant headache for us."

"Sir, whatever the God wills, definitely occurs. No power on earth can stop it. Karei karaavei aape aap, manas ke kichhu nahi haath (It's only the God who is the supreme doer. There is nothing in the hands of man.)" The Giani had said and walked away.

One day, the Giani was sitting in the house of Gurmukh, and Kubir was playing in the courtyard.

"Oi Kulbir don't play towards the cattle. One of them will hit you with his horns," he said to Kulbira.

Kulbir laughed, moved away from the cattle and started running the hand pump.

"How old is he how, Gurmukh Singh?"

"He is in his third year now."

"How fast runs the time! Seems as if it's a matter of days since he was born."

"The sons of Punjab take no time in growing up." Gurmukh Singh was exhilarated in the company of his grandson.

"Sons of Punjab is okay but Punjab doesn't have good time ahead."

"Giani ji, we are also a part of this very society. What can we do in it?

"But relying on a sinking ship and doing nothing looks stupidity to me. A living man does all that he can."

"There is no doubt in it but no solution seems to be in sight. Our government too, is not honest."

In fact, the situation in Punjab was worsening day by day Murders, docoities, extortions etc. had become an everyday affair here. The number of police killings was on the rise. Split between Hindus and Sikhs was increasing. Worse still, effort was on to widen it more by imbuing it with communal tinge. There was clear-cut polarization of media on communal basis.

The central government alleged that arms and ammunition were flowing freely into Darbar Sahib complex through Kar Sewa (voluntary labour) truacks and were being piled there. But why was this in-flow of weapons not stopped, had become a mystery. As per media report, a number of terrorists had made their permanent strategic bases in the holy complex and they were fortifying it well. The headlines of various papers said that all kinds of lethal weaponary was stockpiled in Darbar Sahib complex. The news of army attack to flush out the terrorists from the complex in near future were also in the air. But nobody could say it with certitude as to when this invasion would take place. So far it was the public surmise only.

The people were shaken at the very imagination of an armed attack on the pilgrimage centre of humanity at large.

Gurmukh Singh and Giani Ji were as yet talking when Kuljit came running. He was out of his breath due to running so fast.

"What is the matter Kuljit? Why are you so much afraid?" the Giani asked.

"Giani ji, hide somewhere quickly. The police has again raided to capture you."

"O where shall I hide myself daily? Let them have their will today." The Giani got up to go.

"No Giani Ji, please think a little. You can't believe the police today. They have been given a free hand these days to loot and kill. You are sitting in my house. I won't let it happen like this."

"What can we do Gurmukh Singh? They won't let me rest at peace, I know." The Giani spoke out of sheer dismay.

"Doesn't matter. They will let you off. We haven't done any wrong against the Providence after all Kuljit!"

"Yes, Bapu?"

"You call in Santu."

Kuljit turned away on his feet. Santu's house was not very far off.

Santu came immediately as he got the message.

"Santu, the police has come again to take away Giani ji. You hide him in your house. The police is prone to come here any time due to Kuljit. They have no reason to doubt you for this purpose."

"No no, why all of you invite trouble for me?" The Giani insisted, "You just listen to me."

"We'll listen to you later now Santu!"

"Yes?"

"You run away from behind-through the telian street."

"Let's go Giani Ji."

Santu took the reluctant Giani along like a child who refuses to go to school. Santu's house was situated at the elbow turn of the narrow street. It was a cul-de-sac. That is why the flow of people was very rare and only the members of the families living there could be seen passing through it.

Santu laid a cot behind the cotton bales.

He made his daughter Joginder Kaur aware of all this. Melo was very much frightened at the very mention of police. Joginder Kaur stood in a state of stupefaction. They had a very bitter experience with the police. The pangs of separation from Harpal were still a source of constant agony for Melo.

The police kept running helter-skelter in the village, the whole day like hounds. They cane-charged the innocents, called them names but could not trace their prey.

The Giani kept lying silently on the backside room of Santu's house.

The police had returned empty handed.

The sub-inspector Jang Singh was very much angered at this failure.

"You kept searching him here and there while the Giani was hidden by Santu in his house." The sarpanch Jaggar Singh was telling the police officer in the police-station. "Sarpanch you should have told all this on the spot. Now you have come to show your loyalty to me." The officer vented his ire against the sarpanch.

"I also came to know later on. Otherwise would I have concealed anything from you." The sarpanch felt small. At his heart he abused the incredulity of the S.H.O.

"These police people are really sister-fuckers. They are not the ones to be relied on. The bastard is accusing me just for no fault of mine."

"This Santu too is becoming a hindrance now. Your village won't come on the right track unless taught a befitting lesson," the sub-inspector said with a frowned forehead.

"............" Sarpanch was silent. He had felt insulted.

"Sirpanch ! You do one thing."

"..........." He looked at the officer with interrogative eyes.

"You keep yourself away from your village tomorrow. Then we'll show your village how to dodge the police."

"What will you do?"

"This you will come to know later. But remember my words, if someone dares do such a thing in future, don't call me Jang Singh. Treat me as the offspring of fornication by a scavenger."

"Where shall I go?" The sarpanch failed to think where he could go.

"Go to your in-laws or anywhere else."

"Then I will go today itself. Going tomorrow will create a doubt in the minds of people."

"Send message through someone and don't go back tomorrow."

Early in the morning next day, the police besieged Santu's house. They tied him with ropes and dumped him in the truck.

The truck drove away.

But the police-officer was not contented with this much alone. He perpetrated one more dehumanizing atrocity. He tore away the clothes of Santu's young daughter Joginder Kaur and stripped her naked altogether. The officer himself paraded her in the whole village with his hands cupping her buxom breasts.

The girl was ruined.

It created a shock wave in the entire village. It tantamounted to spoiling the honour of not only Santu, but the whole village. The people sobbed indoors out of shame. The people felt themselves beheaded. Their life was no better than a living death now. The people did not light their hearths out of protest. An eerie silence gripped the air. The spirit of the village seemed to have fled. The aged people wept clasping to each other.

The Giani was not in the village.

The Sirpanch too was not there

Joginder Kaur's mother was having fits. Melo's aged mother Bachint Kaur was sitting helplessly with her daughter and grand-daughter. Her lackluster eyes overflowed with tears. She felt something gnawing at her entrails.

Santu was there in the police station

The people themselves shocked at heart, were trying to console them.

"Has anybody gone for Santu to the police station," asked Jangiro, an old woman all of a sudden.

"Let him die there Amma ji. Will he be one of the living ones when he hears all this? So let him die there." Melo blurted out her desperation at the innocent Santu.

"We too are in no position to show our face to him. Nobody has ever heard what we have been subjected to," Bachint Kaur gave vent to her inflamed feelings. She had never ever thought even in her dreams that man could be so ruthless, barbaric and formidable.

"Even then beti, one must go after him. Nobody can trust police now-a-days. They can go to any extent, we have been."

"Let them kill him Amma ji. Even otherwise we are not among the living ones. Now let it be as it has to be," said Melo.

All the people fell silent.

They could well realize the anguish of Melo.

The sarpanch also came, the next day.

The people of the village approached him in supplication.

"If they wanted the Giani, you should have handed him over to them. Why did you take such a risk and staked the honour of the whole village," The sarpanch rather made the village guilty of all that had happened.

"Don't be so diplomatic sarpanch. From where could we hand over the Giani when he was not here at all?" Gurmukh Singh boiled with rage.

"Even if the police spares us in lieu of the Giani, it's not a losing bargain. So don't let the whole village suffer just for one man. Think calmly and feel the pulse of time." Inspite of being in an odd situation, the sarpanch looked unruffled.

All were silent.

Nobody knew what was good or bad for him. When the Giani came to know, some how or the other, about this savagery, he rushed back to the village.

"I had already been saying repeatedly not to invite trouble for the whole village just because of me......... the Giani cried hoarse His heart and soul-both were bleeding.

"Go sirpanch-tell the police, I have come. Let them crush my bones in a crusher but they should not look at my village.

Tomorrow I will surrender after saying prayer in the Gurdwars. They can take me away anytime they like."

This is what the sirpanch wanted indeed!

He sent a farm-worker to the police-station.

Early in the morning, the Giani started reciting path in the Gurdwara.

The whole village reached fervently.

Degh was prepared

After the usual recitations were over the Giani performed a Kirtan replete with the mood of detachment

Raje shinn mukaddam kutte Jai Jagain baithe sutte

(The kings have become predators and the justice-giver turned into dogs. They spoil the peace of comfortably resting humanity)

Paap ki janj lai kabulhu dhaya, jori mangei daan ve La lo

Saram dharma dui chhap khaloi, koor phirei pardhan ve Lalo

Khoon ke sohile gaaveih Nanak ratt ke kungu pai ve Lalo

(He (Babar) has come from Kabul with a horde of sinners. He has let loose a reign of oppressive taxes in the name of coercive donation. In his regime both propriety and religiosity have hidden themselves somewhere and only the falsehood reigns supreme. That is why Nanak in the form of Lord's beloved, is forced to sing the songs of sanguine by putting the vermilion of blood in the parting of his (her) hair.)

The eyes of the devotees were moistened to hear such notes of detachment.

The Gurdwara was besieged by the police. The siege was laid in a way as if a platoon of some enemy country was positioned in the Gurdwara and which could open canon-fire any time.

After the Kirtan the Giani stood up before the microphone and started saying.

Khalsa Ji[68]! As you know, the police is hunting for me without any fault of mine. They molested Santu's daughter Joginder Kaur only because of me. Now the poor Santu is sitting behing the bars.

Since all this has become intolerable for me, I surrender myself to the police. The police is determined to fulfil its ultimate designs. So let them do what they are up to because when they have defiled the honour of the village, what reason do I have to keep living. Life has become for me a curse. Je jeevei pat lathi jai, sabhi haraam jeta kichh khai. (If living implies loss of honour, then what you eat goes waste only.)

Khalsa ji, my aim was to wean the youths away from addiction and putting them on the Guru's path. The police doesn't like this but now it's for the village as a whole to perpetuate this cause. The Gurbani says: Har nar, muni jan amrit khoj de, se amrit gur te paya (I have got that nectar from the guru which even gods, men, seers etc. keep looking for). So you must tread the Guru's path."

"I may or may not come back alive but all of you must accede to my request. Don't swerve from the right path otherwise we shall be answerable to the guru."

"If I am killed, the onus of looking after Santu's daughter Joginder Kaur falls on everybody in the village. You must give her full support and patronage. After the

Degh is distributed I will court arrest. Khalsa Ji, you must keep your cool. No provocation should be there. It will only give the police another opportunity to unleash a reign of terror on you. So please accept this request of mine alongwith the final Fateh (greeting): Waheguru ji ka khalsa, Wahegur ji ki Fateh.

After this brief speech Giani Pooran Singh took the edict from the holy text:

"My Lord has been so benevolent to me that he has purged my body of five vices plus that of Ego. My Lord has liberated me from the noose of Maya-the illusory world and made heart house the Guru's Shabad. He has not paid attention to any of my merits and

---

[68] A composite address for the congregation of Sikhs.

demerits. He has tied me with the chord of his love and imbued me with His love. O Nanak! Now that I have had a glimpse of that ultimate Beauty by tearing asunder the curtain between us, my heart is filled with bliss. My heart is agog with ecstasy. Now my body has become His dwelling. He has become the master of this House. I have become his servant only."

The Degh was distributed.

The Giani courted arrest.

The whole village stood gloomily, with bated breath.

The trucks of police force drove away.

As they reached the police-station, the Giani was pushed behind the bars.

"Have you come after all, Giani Ji?" said Santu very painfully as he recognized the Giani.

"Yes Santu, the mighty brought me and I came."

"We were destined to meet for the last time Giani ji. I think it will be our last night today," said Santu with his body aching all over.

"You seem to have been tortured a lot," the Giani said as he drew near him.

"Physical torture is different but what the thanedar said in my ears has broken my spirit. Now I am as good as dead." And Santu started weeping bitterly. His tears were streaming over his ears as he was lying on the ground. He was given third degree torture to such an extent that he was not even in a position to move.

"That's why Baba Nanak has called Babar, a tyrant. "Giani ji, now I won't be able to face Joginder and Melo. I want to die very much here." Santu's beard was drenched with tears.

An infuriated Giani was holding the bars of lock-up very tightly.

"Giani ji, I had not ever killed an ant in life. I don't know why such times were in store for me."

" . . . . "

"Oh my God! Why didn't you take me away earlier?"

The Giani's tender heart was torn to shreds. He found it difficult to see the condition of Santu.

In the noon, a drunken Sirpanch Jaggar Singh reached the police-station.

"Come on, sarpanch!" The S.H.O. welcomed him with warmth.

"Thank you, Jang singh." In spite of heavy drunkenness, the sarpanch was speaking in a stable manner.

"We have brought your Giani. He was a straw of your eyes for a long time."

"Wah! Well done," he said and held the police officer in his tight embrace.

"You can talk to him if you like. Tonight we have to send them to the other world. Don't say to me after wards that I had not told you even at their last hours."

"Yes, I'll talk to them."

The sarpanch went towards the lock-up.

"The mother-fucker is drunken in the broad daylight." The S.H.O. chuckled as he told the munshi.

"Such people don't live longer. Let him have his heart's fill for a few days."

"He has nothing against the Giani. Don't know why the bastard is after him.

The sarpanch reached the Giani

"Well Giani, you always kept the village folks under your sway. Now what do you say?" Standing near the lock-up the Sarpanch was in a stagger.

The Giani, utterly surprised looked speechless at the Sirpanch.

The Giani had never thought that the Sirpanch would turn out to be so dishonest and animalistic.

"But sarpanch sahib, I never said anything against you." The Giani had spoken after a prolonged silence.

"How could you do this without having your bones broken? You have made everybody take amrit and turn against Congress. Didn't you fear making Congressmen your enemies?"

"………." Now the Giani understood the whole issue.

"You know who rules the country? And you the handful of people have thought of befooling us."

"…………."

"Now you call whomsoever you like, for help. Tonight, you will be no more."

"God is one for all sarpanch. But you must not remain in an illusion to be a god. Nor should you try to be harnaksha. If He gets annoyed he tears apart with claws, the brutes like you. Still you have time to apologise at the doorstep of God. He is forgiving by nature and going by His nature. He can pardon even the butchers like Sadna and turn them in to adorables."

The Sirpanch laughed with his mouth wide open like that of a yawning wolf. The stench of booze spread all around at once in the air.

"…………." The Giani watched him with great sense of depression.

"Who's this lying near you like a deflated tyre? Is this Santu?

"…………."

"Santu, now you have also tasted the fruit of this Giani's company? Took amrit at his motivation? Now you also face the music."

"Shut up, you devil and get lost!" The Giani stood up with his hands firmly gripping the bars of lock-up.

"Okay, I'm going. How can I afford to come in clash with you Akalis?" The sarpanch said sarcastically and left.

"Hunh……. Shared his feelings? Told you something?" said the S.H.O. twisting one of his moustaches.

"Anyhow, do it tonight… do away with them." The sarpanch said and walked away like an expectant buffalo.

"See, the bastard has forgotten God altogether. Just see the arrogance in his walk and talk." The munshi remarked.

"His end is also not very far off now. Really his days are numbered…." The S.H.O. responded in corroboration.

In the evening a very close friend of sub-inspector Janga Singh came to see him. His closeness was evident from the way he addressed him by the first name Janga only. The S.H.O. met him with an embrace. This more-than-six-feet-statured man didn't look like a gentle man.

"What made you remember me today, Janga?" The man asked with a deep breath. It looked as if the officer was suspended in the lap of this genii-like man with blood-shot eyes and a heavy face.

"I have come immediately after getting your message." Now he released Janga Singh from his bear-hug.

"Just for nothing felt like meeting the friend."

"A white lie altogether!" He said stamping his heavy pounder-like feet on the floor. It made the tenons of the chair groan with excruciating pain.

"We have to terrorise a man." Said the police-officer and looked at his face for a response.

"You just show him to me. I will do it with my eyes only." Saying so he crackled his finger-joints and laughed with a wide-open mouth like a lunatic. A whiff of stench escaped his big jaws and polluted the environment in no time. The officer held his breath then and there. A golden teeth peeped from his rotten plaqued denture.

"For the time being, you have a cup to tea. We'll talk in detail at night." Jang Singh said.

"Is tea a drink to be had? You are talking like a Karaar[69] now. You bring out a bottle and see its magic then." He was talking in a very informal mood.

The officer gave him a bottle and sent him in his upstairs room.

"I couldn't follow your idea of terrorizing?" The munshi asked.

"Should we try him on Giani? May be he gets scared."

"Not at all."

"How?"

"Sir, how can he frighten someone who doesn't break down before the police torture? The Giani has a spiritual support of Gurbani at his back. The Gurbani's force had enabled devotees like Bachittar

Singh tame the inebriated elephant. I wonder what made such a capable officer like you, resort to such ways."

"................." The S.H.O. was really convinced.

"This giant may rather spoil the whole game. First thing, he won't succeed at all- but even if he is able to frighten him a little, he will tell it to, nobody knows, how many people. It will bring us nothing but bad name and leave an impression that the police is important enough to use the private musclemen So sir, feed him well and let him go on his own way."

"So we have brought this wild boar for nothing?" The officer patted his forehead.

"So what? Let him eat and drink well and go. We can use him for some other purpose later on."

"Anyway!" The S.H.O. agreed to the munshi and saw off the man.

---

[69] An Indian community proverbially known for its cowardice and frugal food habits. They are called banias also.

At night the Giani and Santu were eliminated. Their dead bodies were also disposed off.

When on the third day, the panchayat came to enquire about the Giani and Santu, the S.H.O. plainly denied having arrested them.

The sarpanch was not showing any interest at all. The villagers were helpless. Frustrated they returned.

"Sarpanch! Keep them under control otherwise one or two more will have to be done away with. You know the reality." The S.H.O. directed the sarpanch in whisper before he left.

"Don't worry Jang Singh. The whole village is frightened these days. Now, I tell you, nobody will disturb you."

The sarpanch also told the officer before taking leave of him.

When the villagers came to know about the denial by the S.H.O. of the arrest of Santu Giani Pooran Singh, they felt shocked. They were convinced now that the police had killed both of them. So they organized an Akhand Paath for peace to both the departed souls.

The death of Giani Pooran Singh had, in a way, orphaned the village. Two men of flesh and blood had been finished within minutes. A horrifying silence pervaded the entire village. Really, it was a silence of the grave-yard.

Santu's wife Melo and Bachint Kaur would keep weeping all day long by clasping to each other's neck. Their anguish was known to all. The girl, Joginder Kaur would just keep silent. Just like a rock.

Gurmukh Singh and his wife would visit them daily to share their grief and exhorted them to surrender to the will of God. At times, Bunty would also come. She kept talking for most of the time to Joginder Kaur. Sometimes, Kuljit and Bunty would come in the noontime and go back at sunset. Melo and Bachint Kaur least knew what they talked to each other. But they could realize this much that so long as Bunty and Kuljit kept talking to Joginder, she looked quite well. Bachint Kaur and Melo had a sense of relief to see this.

Now Joginder Kaur started reciting Gurbani. She would do all household work. With the effect of reciting from the holy text, she developed a refined intellect and resoluteness.

Going by the last words of Giani Pooran Singh, almost all the people in the village got baptized. The sarpanch Jaggar Singh and amli were the only exceptions.

The baptism added to Joginder's resoulteness still further. She would visit Darbar Sahib twice or thrice a week. Sometimes, Kuljit and Bunty also accompanied her. Then one day-nobody knew under what motivation-she started living in Darbar Sahib. Bachint Kaur and Melo did not feel much about it. Both-mother and daughter-would lead their life together somehow. They had given their land to someone on mutual share basis. A sufficient quantity of grains would reach them and their life was going well.

Gurmukh Singh and his wife would keep enquiring about the well-being of Bachint Kaur and Melo. The visits of Kuljit and Bunty had decreased now.

Punjab situation had become more horrific now. It was marked with clamping of curfew here and there. The incidence of heart-rending shoot-outs had become a daily routine. It was commonly heard that the desperados would come out of Darbar Sahib and after committing the crime would again find shelter in the complex. Nobody could say it for certain what the reality was. The youngmen from the countryside were being arrested at a large scale. Some of them were innocents also. The people were very sad at this state of affairs. The real culprit eluded the police grip while the innocents were being captured and tortured to death.

No side did less in anyway. The question was who succeeded. The whole of Punjab was turned in to a police-cantonment. The outer periphery of Darbar Sahib was guarded by the C.R.P.F. The devotees were subjected to meticulous checking. But still the shoot-out incidents kept happening unabatedly. It was a mystery as to whence the perpetrators came and where did they vanish after all?

Another incident took place in the city.

Jaggar Singh, the Sirpanch and a minion of Thanedar Jang Singh were gunned down and their dead bodies were thrown during nocturnal hours in front of the police-station. The people described it not only as audacity but gallantry as well.

The police took possession of both the corpses and initiated their onward action. Gurmukh Singh's son Kuljit was captured and beaten mercilessly without any fault of his. He was subjected to third degree torture for two days and two nights. He was kept hanging with his hair tied from the ceiling.

When Kuljit's condition worsened, the policemen took him to the hospital.

When Gurmukh Singh came to know about this development he rushed to the hospital. Kuljit was in a semi-dead condition Gurmukh Singh wiped his sweated forehead. The mother tied the hair of her son in to a bun. Plunged in grief, nobody was speaking. Kuljit was lying in a ruthlessly broken shape.

"Shall I bring water for you, my son?" The Bebe asked with an emotion choked throat.

"……….." Kuljit nodded his head in the negative . Some sorrow, some grief, some fury was seething in his heart. He started weeping.

"Why do you cry Beta? God will do good." The Bebe wiped his tears by exercising a little bit of self-control.

Kuljit mustered all his strength.

"Had I been dying after a contribution towards the nation. I would not have felt so aggrieved. But I am going empty handed only. I could do nothing," the spate of tears again gushed out of his eyes as he said this.

"God is very benevolent my son. He will definitely bless you."

"…….." Kuljit was silent.

"Why have you become silent Beta?"

"…………"

"Kuljit……!" The Bebe touched his forehead. It was quite cold. The heartbeat had stopped.

The Bebe cried and wailed aloud.

The doctors came running.

They felt Kuljit's pulse which had stopped.

"He's no more."

The Bebe fell on the deadbody of her son.

Gurmukh Singh stood with a heavy heart. The faces of his daughter-in-law Bunty and the grandson Kulbir were creating a tumult in his mind. He stood non-plussed.

After the post-mortem, the mangled mass of Kuljit's dead body was handed over to the claimants by the doctors. They had sewn back the body with very careless and big stitches.

The cremation of Kuljit rocked and shocked the whole village. Kuljit's widow Bunty was in a very deplorable condition. Kulbir was lamenting the loss of his father. Gurmukh Singh had clasped the grandson to his chest. The anguish of Gurmukh Singh, who was trying to take care of everybody, was inexplicable.

Hardip and his associates had come to attend the cremation just for about half an hour and gone back hurriedly. Nobody knew when police would come and pounce upon anybody.

Prayers were made for the peace to the departed soul in the village-Gurdwara. After the prayers Gurumukh Singh came home with the grandson held in his arms. The death of youthful Kuljit was a great calamity for the family. The icy hand of Death could touch anybody at anytime in the village.

Gurumukh Singh sat hiding Kulbir in his lap as a sparrow hides its fledgeling under its wings. The child had gone asleep after weeping incessantly for long. He was emitting soft snores punctuated with sobs now and then His sobs would cut through the heart of Gurmukh Singh. The helpless grandfather would hardly help wailing at such moments.

Nobody lighted his hearth in the whole village that day. The death of Kuljit in the prime of his youth had plunged the villagers in a dark sea of grief.

Early next morning, the sub-inspector Jang Singh received a phone call. Lost in a wilderness of files he picked up the receiver saying, Hello?"

"Is this Jang Singh on the line?"

"Yes, who's on the other side?" Jang Singh was wonderstruck at the undaunted tone of the caller.

"Thanedara ! You have murdered so many innocents now. We have waited much long. Now you are given twenty four hours to wind up. Eat and drink whatever you like. Meet whomsoever you have to. Your death-warrants have been issued by the Providence. You try to run away wherever you feel like. But you will not see the sun of a day after tomorrow. Be prepared, we have to dispatch you within twenty four hours"

"Who's calling?" said the profusely perspiring officer who otherwise deemed himself no less than a demi-god.

The line was disconnected.

"Who was this?" asked the munshi as he stepped in.

"Don't know who it was. He was threatening on phone but didn't tell his name." The S.H.O. told all this in the same breath. He trembled all over his body like a weaver's warp.

"What such a coward will do who didn't have the courage to tell even his name! Sir, don't be scared of such intimidations. Such threats are the handiwork of miscreants only. They can't do anything at all."

The officer felt his morale boosted a little.

"From where was he speaking?"

"The bloody bastard told nothing at all."

"You take your share of drink and be bold. Don't be afraid of such timid threats. Actually you have not taken a peg or two today. Had you boozed, you would have roared like a lion. In fact, liquor has the capacity to infuse a new life in man."

Acting upon the munshi's advice, the sub-inpector took several pegs one after the other. The drink had emboldened him to brag.

"What harm can these bloody urchins do to me. I am the one to swallow a full man and not to belch at all. They threaten me…..?" Thanedar Jang Singh….?" I can chew them like a piece of radish with the peg. They who threaten me…. I can burn them to ashes even by looking eye-to-eye at them." The drunken cop was speaking very incoherently under the sway of whisky.

In the thick of night he drained a full bottle down his throat and went upstairs to his tenement.

Next day, at about four O' clock in the afternoon, one of Hardip's comrades reached near the gate of the police-station with a hand-cart of vegetables. Two loaded revolvers were hidden under sack-sheet on which vegetables were laid. A twined turban perched on his head made him look exactly like a traditional vegetable-vendor.

Actually, from four O-clock in the afternoon up to eight at night a make-shift vegetable market was a daily feature before this police-station. The vendor who regularly sold vegetables at this very spot was kidnapped by the militants. He was replaced with Harman one of Hardip's accociates. Harman was a very nimble and alert boy. He had gathered the whole information from that vendor.

The policemen did not charge any fees from the vendor for occupying that particular spot and in lieu of this generosity, he gave them vegetables free of cost.

At about five O' clock, a constable came to Harman

"Oi where is Gholu?" he asked.

"Sir his wife is unwell. He has gone with her to the city." Harman said.

"Gone to the city or come to city?"

"Yes, sorry sir, come to the city." Harman corrected himself at once.

"Well go inside and give vegetables to staff in the police-station."

"Sir, I don't know how much of it has to given."

"Ask the cook."

"May I take the rehri (push cart) inside, sir?'

"Go ahead."

"Won't someone stop me?'

"No, you take my name if someone asks."

"Your name, sir?'

"Gurjant," said the constable and went away. Harman pushed his hand-cart in to the police-station.

Crossing the outeryard, he reached near the verandah. His eyes rotated fast in the direction of the office.

The S.H.O. Jang Singh and the munshi were busy chatting to each other while standing in the office and thus out of the range of aim. Herman took the rehri further inside.

When he came back after giving the vegetable, the S.H.O. was standing outside his office.

Harman fished out the weapons.

"Look Thanedara, twenty four hours have not passed as yet and I have come to fulfil my promise," saying so Herman released a torrent of fire and felled the officer like a dry log of wood. All the bullets had hit him.

Other officials nestled in to their places wherever they were, like a cat.

The sentry at the gate opened fire at him but hiding behind his rehri and pushing it wildly out of the main gate, Herman merged with the crowd of the vegetable-market. There stood Hardip, ready to receive him with a motorbike. Harman jumped on to its pillion with the agility of a tom-cat. Both escaped from the spot within the wink of an eye.

The random firing in the vegetable market had created an uproar, making the people run for life in whatever direction anybody could.

The bullet-ridden body of Jang Singh was moved to the hospital where he was declared 'brought dead' by the doctors. Seven bullets were detected to have hit him.

The telephones rang up everywhere in security circles.

This dare-devil incident created an upheaval in the echelons of state power.

Next day, different statements were carried by the newspapers The note of responsibility taken by Hardip's outfit was also published. The responsibility note warned the brutal police officers against their butcherous ways adding that those who did not mend their ways would be eliminated.

All the police-officers were frightened. Their families started urging them with folded hands in the name of children. They asked them not to come in clash with the terrorists.

The heat of the summer was at its peak.

Gurmukh Singh decided to go to Amritsar alongwith his family on the martyrdom day of the fifth Master Guru Arjun Dev. Now his family comprised only Kulbir his grandson, Harpal Kaur his wife and Bunty the daughter-in-law. Melo and Bachint Kaur also got ready to accompany them.

When they reached Amritsar, they found military deployed in such large numbers that when it marched it created an illusion of green crop moving on the roads. The situation was very serious. Each and every movement of the devotees was under scanner.

Gurmukh Singh paid obeisance at Darbar Sahib. When they returned from Darbar Sahib, Gurmukh Singh's glance fell at someone looking quite familiar. He made Kulbir sit on his shoulders and walked briskly towards him.

"Chacha Thamman Singh?" He pressed the shoulder of the old man. The gray-bearded Thamman Singh had not recognized him as he had seen Gurmukh Singh last time when he was yet an unbearded adolescent.

"I am Gurmukh Singh, Chacha! Son of Nidhan Singh Akali."

"Long live, Oi Gurmukha. I had seen you when you were only a teenaged boy with no beard at all….. and now you have………"
Tears seemed to have choked his heart.

"And this boy?" Thamman asked about Kulbir while wiping tears off his eyes.

"My grandson, chacha!"

"Come to me my child, let me bless you," Thamman said to Kulbir with elderly excitement and asked Gurmukh Singh, "How many sons do you have?"

"I had three sons, chacha. Two of them have left for their heavenly abode." Gurmukh became sad as he said this.

"……….." Thamman became silent.

"Anybody else has also come chacha?" Gurmukh himself broke the silence after some time.

"Jaagar has come. He too has grown very old now. Eyesight has become very poor. Sons and grandsons are good for nothing. Liquour, intoxicating pills, tobacco and what not-they have every kind of addiction. He was very said. It was I who asked him to go to Amritsar and pray at Darbar Sahib."

"Now where is he?'

"He is sitting near Jora Ghar[70]. Can't walk much. We shall make him pay obeisance when the crowd of devotees is minimum at night."

"Definitely, we shall do that. We won't let him return disappointed from the Guru's abode."

Hazoor Singh had passed away," told Thamman.

"When?"

"Long back. Had a little fever and then……"

---

[70] A place where the devotees of a temple or Gurdwara leave their shoes before entering the sanctum sanctorum.

Gumukh's wife Harpal Kaur and Bachint Kaur also met Thamman with great warmth.

All of them came to see Jaagar in the Jora Ghar. Jaagar

Started shedding tears of joy at meeting them. They shared their past reminiscences good and bad. It gave them a great sense of relief.

When the crowd of visitors thinned down considerably they made Jaagar pay obeisance at Durbar Sahib. Jaagar showered a rain of blessings on them as a thanksgiving gesture.

When they didn't find any room in Ram Das Serai, they sat outside it in the Parikarma itself with their bag and baggage.

"Chacha ! now come with us to the village and stay there for a week or so. We shall talk to our fill and lighten our minds," said Gurmukh Singh.

"What to do my son, I also feel so much like going with you but the liablilities at home are my chains."

Thus talking to each other they spent half of the night. Sleeping with his grandfather Kulbir was snoring gently.

It was quite hot.

Early in the morning they bathed in the holy sarovar, listened to Gurbani recitation, partook langar and served in the Langar Hall.

They made Jaagar take a bath by giving him support.

The whole day passed very nicely.

At night, the news reached them on the wings of air that military was going to attack Darbar Sahib. Some people thought the military deployment was merely to create fear. A good variety of rumours also percolated in the city. But nobody was ready to believe that army could attack Harimandir Sahib. How could anyone turn against the abode of God?

Darbar Sahib had already been fortified from inside. Now the military had fortified its outer periphery also. This is what signified a bad omen.

On the third of June, the atmosphere was charged with fright. But still nobody expected army invasion.

Outside, the soldiers had fitted their machine-guns and taken positions. Perhaps, they were waiting now for orders from above.

In the afternoon Gurmukha Singh and others came near Guru Ram Das Serai after having had their lunch

At 4 O' clock in the afternoon people heard an announcement being made by the troops. It gave the terrorists nestled inside the Golden Temple Complex, half an hour to surrender their arms and come outside.

The devotees were stunned to hear this. They preferred to keep sitting or standing where they were. Nobody dared to come outside.

The announcement was repeated after two hours But it also failed to evoke any response among the desperados.

At night the power was snapped from outside. The whole complex was engulfed in darkness. Only a faint light glimmer from the Harimandir Sahib or it was just an illusion.

After sometime there was a volley of fire from outside. The devotees lying in the Parikarma were roasted alive.

The deadbodies of Jaagar and Thamman lay scattered outside near the pillar. Terrified with the sound of firing, the children were screaming.

Gurmukh Singh half-lying inside and other half outside the serai was thinking of some method to save Kulbir. He was not worried about his own life.

The firing continued uninterruptedly from outside Sometimes, a canon-shell would also fall in the Parikarma. The devotees were being blown to shreds.

The horrendous night passed.

The sun rose in the East with its usual grandeur.

The whole of Parikarma was drenched with blood. The piles of corpses could be seen around everywhere. The devout visitors were stranded inside and suffered from hunger and thirst.

Gurmukh Singh was shocked to see this horrifying scene. He had clasped Kulbir to his bosom.

There was a great hue and cry all around.

At about ten in the morning, the army again made an announcement asking the terrorists to lay down arms and come outside.

Gurmukh Singh took Kulbir in his arms and walked towards the exit along with his grandson through a street. A terror-stricken Kulbir was not weeping but looking blank out of awe.

Gurmukh Singh kept walking very fast, singing simultaneously.

Paap di janj lai kabulon dhaya

Jorin mangei daan ve Lalo

Saram dharm doi chhup khaloi

Koor phirei pardhan ve Lalo.

The horrid spectacle, to which he was an eye-witness had petrified his spirit. He felt like carrying the heaps of deadbodies on his head.

In the way, he came across a band of soldiers. It sent a wave of shock down his spine.

"Where are you running away, Sardar?" A sepoy with dense moustaches an an ugly pocked face asked him.

"Going to my village sir." Gurmukh tightened the child to his chest. He was very much afraid of death.

"Run away from here otherwise I will shoot you..... ."

"Want Khalistan?" Asked another with his rifle aimed at him. Gurmukh Singh shuddered for a moment. His heart palpitated very fast.

"Leave it yaar. Let the bastard go...."

Gurmukh Singh felt a sense of relief.

"Run away now.... Get lost." The soldier kicked Kulbir. The kick was so ruthless that the child bleated like a goat and his face turned pale with fear.

"No please don't kick the child. Kick me ten times instead." Gurmukh's heart bled at the pain caused to Kulbir.

"Get lost you sons of fornication ! Or otherwise you will be getting everything now and here only." He again lifted his leg at him. But Gurmukh Singh lifted the child and took to his heels. The soldier burst into a peal of laughter.

"The stupids! They always keep demanding something or the other sometime Haryana's water and sometimes Khalisthan."

Suchlike sarcastic comments were hitting Gurmukh's ears. It was just like prinkling salt on the wounds. En route, he had to face hundreds of soldiers.

The whole village wore a deserted look. The army was patrolling in the village also. Every movement had been stopped. Anybody who tried to peep of his own house, could be shot dead. The hungry and thirsty cattle were encircling their mangers restlessness and bellowing.

Gurmukh Singh gave leddoos1 to Kulbir and fresh milk to drink. For the cattle he sprinkled water and flour on chaff. The hungry animals started eating their feed gorgeously. Gurmukh Singh felt eased at heart.

Then Gurmukh Singh made the cattle drink water. Kulbir had gone asleep.

Gurmukh had lost his appetite. He was very much worried about his wife Harpal Kaur and daughter-in-law Bunty.

The night had thickened.

The sound of shells being vomited by the canons in Amritsar were heard here in these villages. The flash of bombs could be seen in the far-off villages also. Whenever there was a dreadful explosion the people would say, Waheguru…. Waheguru."

The Radio was silent.

The supply of newspapers too was not coming.

The television too was mute over the reality of the day.

The whole of Punjab was quarantined from the world. The people had their own surmises about the loss caused to Darbar Sahib. But these were just conjectures, notions. Nobody knew the reality. The people were crazy to think as to what had happened and what was still to come ahead. This much was however certain that people had not ever imagined about what had happened.

The third day had passed by. Harpal Kaur and Bunty had not returned so far. Army-patrolling had been withdrawn from the villages but there was no relaxation of curfew in Amritsar. There were shoot-at-sight orders against anybody found violating the curfew orders.

A frustrated Gurmukh Singh went to Melo's house but was welcomed with a big lock there. So he came back disappointed.

After a full week, Billu a boy from the village reached and the whole village thronged to see him with agreat curiosity.

When he narrated his eye-witness account, it sieved their heart and soul.

"We think several times before demolishing even a small grave! The devils didn't think even twice before demolishing Akal Takht." Waheguru… Waheguru! The elder women of the village exclaimed.

Having freed himself from the visitors. Billu went straight to Gurmukh Singh who was feeding Kulbir at that time. Kulbir's innocent face would make Gurmukh extremely sentimental. With great difficulty, he contained himself.

"Billu, come on?" Gurmukh mustered courage to say. He knew about his coming from Amritsar. Some inner feeling of fear of the unknown or a particular impulse had kept him from going to Billu.

"What a coming on, Taya. A great calamity has fallen. Nobody had ever dreamed of it."

"What God does, Billu, He does for the good of mankind only."

"Attack on Darbar Sahib, Taya?"

"Strange are His ways, my dear. This Darbar Sahib is not demolished for the first time now. It has been ordained by the Guru that it will be broken and rebuilt again and again. So many regimes have confronted it. But whosoever has stood against it, was ruined," said Gurmukh Singh while feeding him the last morsel of bread.

"Taya, any information about Tai?"

"No." Gurmukh's heart thumped very fast at this query

".........."

"You know anything?" Gurmukh was frightened from within. But how could he avoid the bitter reality? And for how long? Truth was truth after all.

"Yes Taya, I know something but it's a very sad information. I'm even afraid of telling it."

"Say my son, say what you have to. Sikhs are used to hear the worst of things. Why do you hesitate?" Gurmukh Singh seemed to have steeled his heart.

"Taya, Tai and Santu's mother-in-law were lying dead near the Darshani Deodhi but Melo Chachi and Bunty Bhabi were still alive. But they were very seriously injured. And moreover, it was a sizzling heat. Nobody was there to shift them to some hospital. So far as I think nobody must have given them even a draught of water."

"We bow to His will, Billu. The fifth Master had said sitting on the hot plate. Tera kia meetha laagei, Har naam padaarth Nanak mangei. (What you do O Lord! Is sweet to us. What Nanak seeks is the name of God only nothing else.) It's His will, my son absolutely His will."

"But Taya, is there any justification for such an oppression?"

"How could you save yourself?"

"God is the only saviour Taya. That evening I lay down in the midst of deadbodies and kept lying there the whole night. The carts arrived in the morning alongwith the scavengers. They must have been asked to remove the dead bodies. The first thing they did was to take away our watches, money etc. and loaded the carts with the corpses like stacks of hay. I was also among them. We were brought in an open space and piled for cremation. There was no arrangement of wood. "Let's bring more corpses and then burn all of the dead together by pouring kerosene on them. They kept drinking near the heap of deadbodies counting the booty snatched from the dead. When they went away, I stealthily slipped out of the corpses and entered the crop. Then meandering my way through the fields, I reached here."

"One thing more Taya." Billu drew quite close to Gurmukh.

"…….." Gurmukh Singh looked at Billu very carefully.

"Santu's daughter, Joginder, you know….?"

"………….."

"The one paraded nude by the Thanedar in the whole village?"

"Yes."

"She herself killed a number of soldiers. She was in Hardip's group."

"What a brave girl!"

"Then, as the troops realized that they were at the receiving end from that side, they threw grenades in that direction and made room for themselves to enter. Otherwise, Hardip and his associates had not allowed them entry into the complex."

"Vah! It means our Hardip too has been killed?"

"Yes, Taya." Billu had a long sigh."

"Anyhow, this worry is also over." Gurmukh Singh said just casually.

"Now only we-the grandfather grandson-are left behind.

"Would you have tea, Billu?"

"No Taya- I won't take tea. Now I will take leave only."

Billu was very surprised to see that Gurmukh had not shed any tears at his son's death.

He milked the buffalo and heated the milk. He always kept Kulbir amused. If he asked about his mother or grandmother, Gurmukh had only one answer to silence him,

"They have gone to the abode of God, my child." Kulbir would become silent to hear this whether he understood something or not. In case he became sad, Gurmukh would say.

"Why do you feel sad. Just see how strong is your grandfather," saying this he would show his biceps to Kulbir and thus make him laugh.

In a way, Gurmukh Singh had become engaged with Kulbira. He would make him take bath, wash his clothes, cook for him and feed him. He would comb his hair and tie them into a bun. He milked the buffalo and then talked to the grandson in his own lisp while playing with him.

"My child, a day will come when the world will narrate tales of your chachas, Tayas and Bapu." Sometimes, he would say to Kulbir. Both-the grandpa and the grandson would sleep on the same bed. At times, he would heave sighs to see the desolation of the house which used to be abuzz with fun and frolic at some time. In such moments his only anchor would be the name of God.

"There are so many people Gurmukh Singh, who are far more miserable than you. Be contented with your grandson," he would say to himself.

When Darbar Sahib was opened for public, the people thronged to it on foot, tractors, trucks, by bus etc.

Although every effort was made to do away with the scars of devastation but still so much of it was clearly perceptible.

Gurmukh Singh burst into sobs at the sight of demolished Akal Takht. Kulbir was looking at his aggrieved grand father. Not only Gurmukh Singh, everybody was weeping.

"Baba ji, why do you weep?" Kulbira asked very innocently.

"The whole world is weeping my child."

"But why?"

"The army has demolished our Akal Takht my dear. That is why......" said Gurmukh Singh with a heavy heart.

"Why did they do so?"

"You won't understand these things as yet. You are a child." Saying this he took Kulbir in his arms.

He lifted the child on his shoulders and came with a heavy mind to the Darshani Deodhi. As told by Billu, Harpal Kaur and Bunty had died at this place. Who could have taken the grievously injured to the hospital.

"Well, you are fortunate enough to have left this barbaric world. May your souls rest at place in heaven." he said. He was not destined to have a last glimpse of his consort who had stood by him through thick and thin. So he took along his grandson Kulbir and boarded a bus for his village. The passengers were talking about this grim tragedy which had claimed numerous human lives. Everybody had his own woeful tale to narrate.

"What did they do with the dead bodies lying in Darbar Sahib," Gurmukh Singh asked the man occupying seat next to him.

"They were piled together and burnt by pouring kerosene on them. What else they were to do, Baba?" In a way, he was making fun of Gurmukh Singh's absurd question.

Gurmukh Singh kept silent.

Immediately after alighting from the bus, Gurmukh reached the village Namdardar[71] "Welcome Gurmukh Singh!" The Nambardar met him with warmth.

"Thanks Nambardar Sahib." Gurmukh said and sat before him.

"Well, what can I do for you?"

---

[71] Village headman.

"My land and house are for sale. Tell me if there is some customer."

"Why? What for? Do you plan to go somewhere else?" An astonished Nambardar asked so many questions in a single breath.

"Yes." Gurmukh said and came back.

When he reached home, he was shaken to see the desolation pervading all over. This was the house where Gurjit, Hardip and Kuljit had played together. Bunty had come here as a bride. Harpal Kaur's loud accent used to reverberate in the atmosphere- where has all that gone? It has vanished like a dream.

"Baba ji!" Kulbir pulled Gurmukh Singh out of his world of past memories.

"………." Gurmukh Singh was startled at once. He looked at him but his vision was blurred due to the film of tears covering the eyes.

"Yes Kulbir?" Gurmukh felt something biting at his entrails when he saw the stupefied face of the child.

He picked Kulbir and said.

"We shall go somewhere else from here?"

"Yes, my child."

"Why?'

"Those who ever lived here with us will always keep possessing us if we don't leave this place."

Gurmukh Singh started weeping again.

"The bonds of love donot leave you so soon dear child. Although they have left us forever but they still live here…….. here in my heart." He said with tearful eyes.

"………….." Kulbir was looking at his grandfather's face. He couldn't understand much of what the old man had said.

"My child! This village has not been loyal to us. We shall go to Delhi where the ninth Master had taught mankind the difference between living in the real sense of the term and just passing life. Don't worry we both-grandpa and grandson-shall live together."

".................."

"Come on, beta Let us start preparing food. Then we shall sit together and recite Bani."

Klubir started peeling garlic.

Gurmukh started pounding spices into paste.

Gurmukh Singh had hardly placed the cauldron of Dal in the Hara when Panchayat came to his house. The villagers had elected a new sarpanch with unanimity. He was a baptized Sikh

"Are you all right Gurmukh Singh?"

"I'm fine, you Panchayat members! Please come on let me prepare tea for you."

"No, we won't take tea. We have to share something with you."

"Yes, please say what service can I do for you?" He bowed before the Panchyat with all veneration.

"What do you think about Santu's house? The whole of his family is killed. The Panchayat says we should talk to you as he was very close to you."

"Panchayat's decision is my decision. I am not without you?" Gurmukh Singh said with all humility.

"Panchayat has decided that Santu's house should be turned into Gurdwara by installing Nishan Sahib there. What do you feel? It will facilitate the people of this locality.

They have to go a long way to pay obeisance in the main Gurdwara."

"It's a very good idea. I a gree to all of you."

"Okay then. Let it be executed tomorrow itself."

The decision was made and the Panchayat left. Billu came to Gurmukh Singh.

"Taya?"

"Yes?"

"Amli's condition is very poor. You must go to him. He remembers you."

"Amli has been unwell for several days."

"Seems, he will breathe his last today."

"You do one thing. Sit with Kulbir and I am going to enquire about amli's health for some time."

"Go Taya." I am sitting with Kulbir."

Gurmukh Singh left.

A bundle of bones now, the amli was lying soaked with sweat all over his body, in a corner of the cot.

Gurmukh went to him and pressed his hand. This gesture made amli's eyes streaming with tears. With a signal of his hand he asked Gurmukh Singh to draw near him. Gurmukh sat on the floor near his cot.

"Gurmukh Singh! I will leave today.' He relapsed into tears as he said.

"Why do you feel sad?" Gurmukh also felt gloom gripping his mind. The lively and vivacious amli looked grief incarnate today.

"Listen to me carefully."

"Yes?"

"I could not take amrit. It was my bad luck to have addiction overpower me."

" . . . . "

"You must hold a Paath in my name after I die- May be he forgives me."

"God is very forgiving, don't worry. You have repented for your omission, so he will definitely shower His grace on you. If He is up to forgive. He blesses even a demon like Kauda. Gurbani say.

Jinmanas se devte keeye, karat na laagi var (He who has turned men in to gods, takes no time in forgiving). He is infinite."

A wheezing sound started coming from the throat of amli. It was a sign of imminent death. So Gurmukh Singh began to recite Gurbani near his ear.

"Jaha mata pita sut meet na bhai

Mann uha naam terei sang sahai."

(He who has no parents, offspring or friend, only His name O jiva will stand by you)

Amli breathed his last.

Gurmukh closed the eyes of the deceased reciting Waheguru."

The whole village joined his cremation.

"He had expressed the last wish that a Paath should be held in his name." Gurmukh told the sarpanch.

"We'll do it in Santu's house itself."

"Well said."

The people of the locality where Santu lived, voluntarily dusted and cleaned Santu's house, removed the cobwebs and even washed the floors.

After collecting the mortal remains of amli, as last-prayer Sehaj Paath was held in Santu's house and a Nishan Sahib[72] was installed.

Before the Bhog ceremony, Gurmukh Singh sold off his land and house to the Nambardar. Pocketing the amount, he sent a message to Billu who appeared at once.

"Billu, do you know someone in Delhi?"

"Enough of it Taya. May Maasi from Baranal lives there alongwith her family. They have their transport business in Delhi."

"We'll go to Delhi, my son."

---

[72] Sikh flag

"Why Taya?"

"For children, one has to do a lot. I will get Kulbir admitted in to a very good school. Studies will make his career. What's here in the villages now? Either face humiliation at the hands of police or spend nights in lock-up. He will become sensible in city-life. Moreover without him what do I have to do for! Will spend the rest of my life like this only."

"You are right Taya. There is nothing in village to feel like living there. I will definitely help you, the way you like. My Maasad[73] enjoys great influence there. I will go with you whenever you ask me."

"We shall leave after amli's Bhog ceremony. Let's not talk much about this programme. If the village fraternity gets to know this, they won't let us go. One has to do much for the children. I am also breaking myself away from the village just because of Kulbir. Otherwise, who would leave his own people." Gurmukh Singh became very sentimental.

"I can feel your agony Taya. Don't worry. I will stand by you as long as possible."

"Nice of you, my son."

Billu left.

After Amli's Bhog ceremony was over, Gurmukh Singh handed over the key of his house to the Nambardar and pocketed the price amount safely.

As he stepped out of the house with Kulbir, his heart sank. He felt the departed kinsmen calling him. The doors and walls seemed to be stopping him by wailing mutely. But for the sake of his grandson, Gurmukh bore all this.

"Come on my son."

Billu, Gurmukh and Kulbira set out towards the bus-stand. Gurmukh Singh's heart bled for the love of his roots. Billu was silent with a feel of his anguish.

---

[73] The husband of maasi (Mother's sister)

They boarded the bus and reached the nearby city from where they were to sit in the train for Delhi. They sat in a tea-shop to take a cup of tea. He ordered a glass of hot milk for Kulbir.

"Eat or drink whatever you like now. You won't find anything to eat in the way." Gurmukh told Kulbir.

He had hardly made the payment to the shopkeeper, when a commotion was heard from the railway station. Many a police constable were running after a captive with long and strong sticks in their hands. The captive would sometimes start laughing and then start weeping.

"What's all this about, friend?" Gurmukh Singh asked the shopkeeper.

"Just telling. Let the situation calm down a little. Will tell you everything."

The policemen had overpowered the man. He was rolling on the ground, panting hard at the same time.

"He seems to be a lunatic."

"Yes he is."

The police took away their captive.

"Now, listen Sardar Ji," the shopkeeper said," This captive used to be a constable in Punjab Police. You must have heard of Bedi, the advocate? He was a very famous lawyer."

"Yes.........."

"This constable had killed Bedi's family. Bad deeds bring retribution on you very much here in this world. He didn't spare even his small boy. He did kill the child but it had a rocking impact on his mind. Then throwing tantrums like a mad man, he himself approached the court to surrender. The court sent him to jail. Now the police men carry him for witness in the court. The judge refuses to record his statement due to his abnormalcy. He has a brutal strength in him. The police men find it very hard to control him. One day he hit his own head with a brick. A jet of blood gushed out of his head but he was laughing at the sight of his own blood. Both the jail staff and policemen are very sick of him. The policemen tell me something about him when they come here for a cup of tea. The policemen sometimes let him off deliberately."

"Why so?"

"So that he may create a scene and they may tell the judge that he is still having fits of lunacy."

"But there must be some reason for this?"

"Sardar ji, they are afraid lest in a state of normalcy he should make any statement before the judge which may unveil the real faces of the police officers."

"That is also right."

"When he killed Bedi's son, he was under the influene of liquor. But when the effect of booze vanished, his head turned to think. "What wrong had the small child done to me that I finished him-the image of God?"

"............"

"It's said that when he was about to kill the child, he ran for life, crying and screaming and this devil chased him, caught and then shot dead. Sardar Ji, heaven and hell are nowhere else they are very much here. Now you see his condition his children are ruined and his own life is no less than a living death." The shopkeeper concluded the whole story.

"Come Taya, let's buy tickets."

They bought tickets and boarded the evening train. They reached Delhi in the morning. Kulbir had made all his journey in sleep. Billu and Gurmukh too had a nap but the slain lawyer Bedi and his innocent son were always sitting heavily on Gurmukh's heart. He had completed his entire journey with Kulbir clinging to his chest.

Having reached Delhi, they hired an auto-rickshaw and reached the house of Billu's masi. His massad was a very amicable and vivacious man-quite seasoned. During youth, he had worked as a truck-driver and after his father's death he had sold his land and purchased trucks in Delhi. He moved among the men of substance. Drinking before going to bed at night and having opium after getting up in the morning was his daily routine. He was also fond of calling names to the drivers after drinking but nobody uttered a word before him. To sum up he had a prestigious position in the society.

"Deposit the money in bank, Sardar Ji. The very interest will be sufficient for your expenses." Billu's maasad Bikkar Singh said.

"As you wish maasad ji. Taya is a very close family man to us. I have already told his story. They are only two of them grandfather and the grandson. You buy them a workable house and put the rest of the amount in a bank."

"Don't worry Sardar Ji. This is your own house. We shall do the needful within a day or two. I know a lot many of the property dealers. This is my responsibility now. Leave it all on me."

"We have come to you with grace of God."

"Don't say anything more now, please."

The whole family of Billu's masi was very loving and affectionate. In spite of being a hardcore Bacchenalian, Bikkar Singh was a man of firm determination. Whatever he said, he would do it at costs. His drivers would call him 'bharthu' (Tempest) or bhamakkar (a moth) at his back. But they were very much impressed with his generosity. They were proud of him.

Within a week Bikkar Singh arranged a good house for Gurmukh Singh in a peaceful area. He introduced him to the neighbours. Kulbir was admitted to a school. Ration was also purchased in sufficient quantity.

Life had once again come on the rails. Kulbir started going to school. Gurmukh dropped him there and picked him up as well in the afternoon daily.

Bikkar Singh would also visit him off and on, shared his weal and woe and arranged grocery etc. for him. When in need, Bikkar Singh would go and withdraw money from the Bank. All the bank officials had become familiar with the polite and gentle demeanour of Gurmukh Singh.

On holidays, Gurmukh Singh would take Kulbira to Bangla Sahib Gurdwara. It instilled in them a new faith for life.

Gurmukh Singh's new house had a triveni before it. It was a trinity of baniyan, peepal and neem. Gurmukh would make Kulbira pour water in its roots daily.

Before taking meal he would ask Kulbira.

"Watered the triveni?" Receiving a yes from Kulbira, he would go out and stand near the roots of the triveni.

"Meditators! How are you? Are you happy?" He would ask the trinity aloud. Then taking their silence as 'yes', he would say, "Well! Long Live ! Enjoy yourself! Okay, now I am going to my bed. You too go asleep" and himself go to his bed.

Early in the morning, Gurmukh would again go to the triveni. Having completed his Paath he asked them," How was your night?"

The days were passing in a fine way.

The grandfather, grandson and the triveni were quite mixed up with each other. They were each other's support.

Gurmukh Singh would keep sitting under the triveni till the school hours were over and talk to it. It amused him and thus was a good pastime.

It was 31 October, 1984

A very ominous news came.

The Prime-minister Indira Gandhi had been assassinated by her Sikh body-guards. A shock wave permeated the whole atmosphere The blood forsook the Sikhs settled in and outside Delhi, in other states.

The bloodletting of Sikhs started in the whole capital. The similar was the state of affairs in other states as well. The Sikhs were being pulled out of their homes and killed.

But Gurmukh Singh was unaware of all this.

Hiw neighbouress Parvati came running to him shouting, "Baba ji. Baba ji!"

"What's the matter my daughter?" The Baba sitting under the triveni got up on his feet in consternation.

Baba ji, someone has killed Indira Gandhi. The rioters are killing the Sikhs. You hurry up and bring Kulbira back from the school."

"Indira Gandhi is killed by someone. But why are they killing the Sikhs," the Baba was confounded to think over the prevailing situation.

"Baba ji, you can't understand. You bring back Kulbira soon. Indira is killed by the Sikhs, so the rioters are killing the Sikhs to avenge. You rush off, hurry up."

The Baba ran towards the school in bewilderment.

Some new strength was infused in him. He was greatly worried about Kulbira.

A tumult was created in the school. The Sikh parents had thronged to take along their children. The Hindus had no such threat to face.

The Baba called the grandson aloud saying, "Oi Kulbira" He was panting hard for breath.

When he saw Kulbir, he lifted him on his shoulders and left the school premises as fast as he could. Not only Gurmukh, all the Sikh parents were under going this harrowing situation. They were eager to collect their wards and run off.

The Sikhs were subjected to persecution the whole day long. The girls and women kept being molested. Their properties were set ablaze and burnt to cinders. Only humanity kept crying.

Nobility or righteousness had vanished somewhere and vice ruled the roost.

On third day Parvati came to Gurmukh Singh.

The Baba was sitting with Kulbira hidden in his lap.

"Baba ji, you come to my house. We are Hindus. So nobody will doubt us."

"Parvati, If death has to come, it will come to me at your house also. Let God be merciful. Forces of darkness are reigning supreme everywhere."

"Baba ji think at least about Kulbira if not about yourself. My husband has asked me to take you to our house.

Now Gurmukh Singh, picked up Kulbira and walked with her.

The capital was in smoke. The flames had touched the skies and descended. Property worth crores had turned into ashes. The virgin girls were treated by the ruffians as prostitutes. Almost every street felf suffocated in smoke. The Sikhs were being finished on pick and kill basis. "Kill…. Murder……….eliminate…." had become the chant of the day. Killing and rampage was the common scene, everywhere in the national capital. The riff-raff of society treated it as a godsend opportunity, not only to wash their hands but dye them also in the flowing Ganges of hatred.

The night thickened.

The irate mobe attacked Gurmukh Singh's house. They ransacked it altogether.

The Baba and Kulbir were sitting with bated breath in Parvati's house. The mob. Was shouting joyously. Parvati and her husband Ram Partap were looking at this rowdysm while standing at their door.

"The Sikh is not seen anywhere?" Someone from the frenzied mob said.

"But the traitor lives very much here," said someone.

"Sure?"

"What you talk yaar1. I am sure."

"Then where has he run away?"

"Might have escaped."

"Ask these neighbours."

"You slut ! Where has the old man gone?" One of them asked Parvati who was boggled at this impudence.

"We don't know." She replied scarily and ran inside.

"This bitch must have hidden the bastard. Let's search him in her house." The mob barged in to the house. They thrashed Ram Partap so badly that he became unconscious.

"Fuck this bitch. She has sympathies with the Sikhras."

Many drunkards made Parvati fall on the floor. They tore away her sari and started biting and plucking at her body. Parvati's shrieks were lost somewhere in the boisterous and diabolic peals of the rascals' laughter. Ram Partap had probably died. Bathed in blood he lay prostrate in the courtyard.

The Baba could no longer put up with this animalism.

He came out of his hide-out and roared like a lion with a sword in his hand,

"O scoundrels! Why are you showing your manliness on a helpless woman….. Face the Guru's Singh now." Saying this he wounded so many of them with this sword.

"Hold the bastard. He has nearly killed me," cried a man with an ugly face. Blood was streaming down his arm.

"Oho, he has killed me also!" another bleated. A jet of blood was flowing out of his temple.

But how long the lone old man could resist the frenetic horde. How far he could fight.

The provoked mob over powered him.

The Baba was panting restlessly even in their grip like a lion who would pounce upon them just given little more of a chance.

"Burn alive the grandson of this dog before his eyes," decreed one of them. He was trying to stop the flow of blood from his waist cut open by the Baba's sword.

The incited mob brought out the child Kulbira and made him unconscious with the blows of fisticuffs, kicks etc. The Baba was in the grip of some others.

The unscrupulous mob poured kerosene on Kulbira and set him afire. The flames flew to the skies at once. Kulbir groaned with pain but the Baba started reciting with his eyes closed.

Tera keeya meetha laaga

Hari naam padaarath Nanak mange.

Tears dripped from his eyes unabatedly.

The mob kept clapping and shouting with joy at all this sordid play of gore and fire.

The Baba kept reciting "Tera keeya meetha laage….." till Kulbira was burnt completely and stopped as the fire extinguished. When the goons loosened their grip, he collapsed on the floor.

"This bastard too is gone," said one of them while hitting the fallen oldman's head with a heavy iron-rod.

"Leave now…." the leader of the rowdies commanded. The mob left the scene.

Parvati lay dead in the courtyard-stark naked. Blood oozing out of her cheeks and breasts had congealed but it was still flowing from her lower part.

Next day, the Baba regained his consciousness and found himself in the sees Ganj Gurdwara. Countless people sat there laden with their miseries. Someone was weeping while some injured one had his face contorted with excruciating pain.

Some pious-looking man, highlighted the importance of sacrifice in the presence of Guru Granth Sahib, saying:

"Brethren ! Had Guru Gobind singh not made supreme sacrifices, we would never have known the art of life. Had he not sacrificed his family, we would never feel the strength obtained from bowing before His will. Had Christ not been crucified, Christianity would not have spread so far and wide in the world. Similarly, if Buddha and Mahavira had made sacrifices, their followers would have been not thirty lacs, but thirty crores today...."

These words gave a lot of strength to the spirit of Gurmukh Singh. He folded both his hands and appeared like a petitioner before Guru Granth Sahib, praying.

"Lord! Going by the citation' Teri vast tudh aagei raakhei, (I surrender what was yours to you) this servant of yours contributed towards his faith according to his mite with your grace. Be kind enough to accept it at your doorstep. I look forward to come to this world again in human garb, become your slave and serve you what has remained incomplete in this life....."

"O Lord ! Man is prone to err but you are a great Forgiver. I am the sinner and you are the Redeemer. So be kind to forgive, if this child of yours made any mistake intentionally or unintentionally in life........" Praying thus, the Baba lay down prostrate before Guru Granth Sahib in obeisance but could not get up on his feet again.

There was a long queue of devotees behind him.

"Get up, you devotee of the Guru! There are so many people waiting for their turn," someone said shaking the oldman's shoulder. But how could the Baba answer. He had completed his temporal journey.

The devotees removed him from the presence of the holy scripture, gave him a bath in the Gurdwara itself. From the receipts lying in his pockets, they knew about his address.

The neighbours told that the Baba was passionately attached to the triveni. He used to talk to it and share his joys and sorrows.

So, the Baba was cremated on one side of the triveni.

Feeling pangs of separation from both - Baba Gurmukh Singh and Kulbira-the triveni was very sad today. Extremely crestfallen. As if it was orphaned without the Baba. Yes, orphaned!